The Lent Hand

Adventures in Beach Town Towing

Kathleen K.

Also available by the author:
All Age – General Fiction
Joody – A Case Study in Post Dramatic Stress Disorder
ISBN 145633655X

Adults Only – Sexotic pot-centric fictional memoir
Stoner with a boner (It's a Long Story)
ISBN 1463583680

Copyright © 2011 Kathleen K.
All rights reserved.

ISBN: 1466220155
ISBN-13: 9781466220157

The Lent Hand

a/k/a

Jeromeo to the Rescue

Book I – The Lent Hand   *1*

Book II – Family. Life.   *81*

*Dedicated to the man
who had the happy wife.*

Book I – The Lent Hand

You gotta love your mother. That's a rule of nature for which my mother should be grateful. Back in 1970, she was living on a commune in Oregon, pregnant by one of several potential donors, unhappy with the state of the planet although she appreciated having a position upon it. My mother was not sure whether to give the baby me to a nice couple of bikers who'd stopped in for a few months – she abandoned that idea when they couldn't imagine a suitable sidecar for the biker-lady plus baby (ahh, fate). Instead, my mother decided that she would live the straight life our last trimester together. She went home to her mother's husband's house to eat their healthy food, sleep in her own clean bed, and give birth to me in a hospital with all its "establishment" implications. She did this for my sake, not for herself, because it seemed to her as if I had a life of my own even as I inhabited her physically. I was a foreign body, temporarily tolerated.

This natural "love your mother" law was easier for my mother because *her* mother was kind and caring. I should know because Grandma raised me. My step-grandfather decided that my mother was his wife's daughter and his wife's daughter's kid was not his responsibility: he could not say yes or no to my living there because the decision was beyond him. Carl Lewiss was not a mean man, he wouldn't take the time to be; he was consumed with maintaining his daily habits. He married my grandmother, Eileen Hampton Clover Lewiss, after she was widowed and left with a teen-age daughter (who not long after lit out for her hippie destiny). Carl had waited for Eileen for many years, after the death of his first wife of whom we never spoke. He waited, knowing that he would outlast Ernie Clover and win Eileen in the long run. My "real" actual grandfather Ernie was a drunk, unemployable except as a shanty guard at a little-used dock owned by a cousin. My grandmother sewed for money then and now; my earliest memory is watching her foot on the sewing machine pedal, lightly coaxing even stitches out of the old Singer. She cut and stitched fabrics too rich for her to own. I eventually figured out my "real" grandpa had fallen into the river and drowned, his body found many miles downstream before anybody was sure he was actually missing (that is, gone against his will, he was known to move off for days or weeks at a time). He was not a frequent topic of conversation any more. For better or worse, Grandma stayed with him until death did them part. And he was departed.

My mother's name is Helen but she insists on being called Starlight. Even thirty years after the first stage of her nomad lifestyle flared away during late-stage pregnancy, giving birth, newborn care, she felt a growing realization she was her father's daughter... hitching to Woodstock hadn't caused her to turn wild, she went to the festival because she was already on the road. Starlight Clover liked to party, she liked to disappear, she liked to be FREE. I hear I slipped out on a few jaunts when I was still small enough to tuck into a papoose-type carrier and allow her to hitchhike, but once I needed a stroller I ruined her chances for catching a ride. The first time she left me behind I was too small to care and by the time I could care, I didn't. Grandma was there and she was life to me. Grandpa Carl was like the horses, things to be admired from a distance but they might bite and kick if you got too close. I was smart enough to retain that information and so my little boyhood was lived in a peaceful household. Grandma took care of Grandpa Carl and she took care of me. He ate first, I went to bed first; she gave us both baths. She had regretted not having more children and considered me a bonus. When she had realized just how useless Ernie Clover was going to be as a husband to her and a father to their daughter, she took care not to have another child. It was one of the deep regrets she had about staying married to Ernie. She hadn't had her name on the title to a house until she married Carl Lewiss, she needed that kind of deep rooting to be able to reach out to the community as far as she did. Half her sewing was for charity, a deluxe wedding dress at a sacrifice price for a poor bride, special jumpsuits for the Quinlan boy who'd lost half his left arm to a horse bite (more on that later). The money-work was fine tailoring of business ladies' suits, and creating evening dresses for the society set. Financially secure in her second marriage, she was able to enjoy me.

Starlight came and Starlight went, sharing legal custody of me with my grandmother to make medical matters and other official actions simpler. It was hard for Eileen to understand her daughter but she had accepted Ernie's need to do what he felt he should do and so it was with Starlight. And so it is with me.

Carl and I didn't dislike each other, we were always <u>always</u> cordial. He provided shelter to me and as long as I respected that fact then everything was fine. In his house, clothes were put away promptly and dishes were done after every meal, appliances wiped down, floor swept; no backtalk. Starlight toned herself down during her visits and, in fact, it was understood she originally left to avoid inevitable conflict with her mother's old-world husband. She couldn't stand to see her mother fetch "that man" his evening cocktail, she missed her own father although she hadn't really known him well because he was drunk or gone most of the time. She couldn't admit that her father's care-less life made her mother have to work harder at supporting them all. She thought her mother sewed because she loved it but I knew better, it was Grandma's lifeline and she became part of the machine when she sewed; what she loved was her people.

I went to college thanks to Carl, he had invested some money in my name and let the market dictate my return (more fate); having done that as a gesture for my grandmother, he set aside all thoughts of further planning for my future. My grandmother had her own college fund for me and she earmarked part of her sewing income to feed it. I would go with her to the Savings & Loan and we'd buy more shares for my account. It was a lesson in long-term accumulating. Carl didn't watch my stocks and so I had only a vague idea of what the stock market was or the impact it would have on my future; my rising balance in the savings and loan made sense to me then. They both make sense to me now.

I loved earning interest and kept special note of it, since I considered it a fascinating aspect of saving. Not only did you get back all the money you put in, you got rent on the money they held for you! Hey, OK. I got an allowance based on chores so it was an easy lesson to work quickly to minimize my own labor since the pay was fixed no matter how long I took to do it. Don't make a big deal out of a job, do it and let it go. I raked tons of leaves, I carried out pail after pail after pail of kitchen garbage, I swept the porch a minimum of 104 times a year (Saturday and Wednesday). I didn't question if this was fair, this was the way it was at the Clover-Lewiss household. Starlight even pitched in when she was home; she liked to do specific projects like polishing the silver or organizing Grandma's fabric supplies. She wasn't much good on daily maintenance (or personal hygiene). I liked her well enough although she did not behave in a way that I could understand when I was younger. I remember wondering, when I was about seven, hadn't she read the books where the mommy is always there? Couldn't she read them now and get the message? I was so well tended by my grandmother that all of this was theoretical, I didn't need to be rescued, I didn't dream of a regular family because I was so thoroughly aware that this was my one and true family. Still, I knew my mother should have been there and she opted not.

As an adult I deposit money for Starlight every month at the co-op bank she uses when having to deal with the real world; I started that when I got out of college. My sophomore year at State, she'd come up with $10,000 (she said it was the residual value of her share of the original commune when it disbanded and they sold the land, maybe it was). Carl was favorably impressed because there weren't any strings attached. She was funny that way, finding the real world an interesting place to hang out for a while, appreciating the customs of its citizens enough to visit but not to stay. When I got my first job, I bought her a personal medical insurance policy that included the sorts of homeopathic providers she preferred.

After a few years I added $250 a month for out-of-pocket health maintenance expenses. We had agreed this was a sensible way for me to express my ongoing concern for her welfare. In her maturity it bummed her out that she had missed so much of my childhood. She'd eventually gone the way of AA so I listened to her earnest atonement, wondering if she would ever understand that she was honored for her role but not respected for her performance.

 I get a business degree and my first job is great. I'm hired to manage a three-site chain of batting cages, to do the books and run the payroll. They told me they were marginal at best and needed to either invest more or pull out. If I'd give it a year, they'd see what could be done. It took me about a month to figure out we didn't have an image, and that we had the wrong people behind the counter. Too many jocks, not enough geeks. The average batter isn't looking to be intimidated at the counter; it is primarily a rental function after all, prompt (correct) calculations are valued. On the other hand, the cage area had to be roamed by athletes who could and would offer practical demonstration of stance and connection. I had the places painted inside and out to set a new tone, we posted clear signs. We had bigger waiting rooms built with toy yards for little kids so big brother or sister could bat for thirty minutes without mom/dad and the brats hanging around too close. The partners had originally invested in good equipment and I got some grease-monkeys from the junior college shop classes to work part-time under the supervision of a retired mechanic. With the spruced up facilities, we were doing more business. The insurance was high but we were careful to follow every safety rule and city/county/state/federal code we could find. Batting helmet and a gladiator pad on the exposed arm were required (fiddling with these kept you busy while you waited your turn). A compulsory ten-minute video for new members showed how the cages worked, how to set the speed and strike zone; you got a bat key chain engraved with your name to streamline the check-in (geeks are good engravers and it fills the wait time). Lose the chain? Watch the video again to get another. The junior cages couldn't throw faster than forty-five, the adult cages (when tuned) tried for eighty. I made a deal with the local kids' leagues for team rates off-season.

From a marketing point of view, I got the cages mentioned in the paper more often; we started a gear exchange and that gave the staff something to do between customer rushes. Donated uniforms were washed, measured, tagged and sorted into small bins by color and type. Baseball shoes (soft cleats only) were washed in a germicidal solution; if they couldn't survive one spin cycle they weren't sturdy enough to pass on. We provided measuring tape and a Personal Stats form to fill out so the customer could know their own measurements and match them to the tags. It seemed best to tote up the new numbers on each visit. We didn't use size numbers because those were inconsistent, we matched the dimensions of arm length and shoulder width and called it wingspan. All pants were waist x inseam. No dressing rooms, it was an exchange after all and if the item didn't work out just pass it on or trade it for something else. We found that effort created meaningful involvement with the community we were trying to reach: kids and people who cared about kids. The grown-up batters motivated themselves because it was their specific interest. We had a sponsor board for the donors to our employee scholarship fund. A local shoe chain donated a hundred pair of athletic socks. I had fun for a few years, starting programs and making money at the same time, watching kids blast back at the pitching machine, facing down their Randy Johnson, shouldering the bat against that demon sixth grader in the church league.

It wasn't only kids who wanted time in the cages. There were diehard players of every age, tuning up for city league teams and annual family face-offs. I spent a little time in the cages too, ostensibly for quality control, but obviously I liked connecting with the ball. The contact ran up my arms and into my imagination, the ball was flying over the wall at Fenway, rocketing down the third base line, arcing higher than even Cameron can leap. I got talked into playing for a local computer sales company who batted weekly at our cages. These people were SERIOUS and drove themselves at practice, in-season and off. I kept it up for a few years but over time it felt like I was back in high school. I was playing OK but I wasn't dreaming of dropped third strikes. The level of fitness was a notch above my own goal and so I took the opportunity of leaving the job to resign from the team. Luckily, the fitness lingered.

I came out of that deal with a bit of money and felt that was just about as close as I cared to get to public service. I found many of the client family units defective, parents under pressure, kids venting the family toxins. I liked the money, but not enough to stay more than a few years, because it was fun to build it up and tinker with its operations but boring to repeat it day after day after day…

I tried a city job (recruiter in a contract engineering firm) but it damn near killed me. I was knocked off the curb at a busy corner by a bicycle messenger then was clipped in the hip by a city bus – but I wouldn't have *been* on the corner except for that job. I got a hefty settlement so I thought it was a sign to take time out. My thirties were looming; I saw that horizon. My post-accident self-prescribed physical therapy was walking the ocean shore, strolling down the small streets to the water's edge (wherever that happened to be on any particular day). I struck out for distance, using the sand as resistance and as cushion. I had a pedometer and was faithful to a four-mile round trip. It was my excuse for moving there from the big bad city, after all. I had purchased a small cottage about a quarter-mile from the beach because it was all on one floor with a big fireplace and a useful kitchen. I found a bed that sat on a pedestal of drawers so I eliminated the need for a dresser (and made the bed high enough for me to get in and out easily), I put a writing table and chair in the corner where the dresser would have been (I had the matching chair out in the great room to make a table for two). The hip replacement has scotched baseball from returning to my agenda. Maybe after a few years I could probably trot the bases but I'd never feel the power coiling from my feet up through my body and out my arms into the bat. Not like I did before I was remodeled. One doctor referred to the accident as an "insult" to my body and I couldn't have found a better word for it.

I started playing cards with some local beach folks, Aidan (the hardware-feed guy), and his fellow merchants. I suppose it was understandable that with money in the bank I felt little motivation to work in the traditional sense. Living the non 9-to-5 lifestyle was accepted in the beach community as a matter of personal choice not to be probed too deeply by others. I was talked into buying a truck over the course of several weeks of low-stakes gambling. In fact, I liked the feel of the pickups I'd ridden in (with high-end shocks) and it wasn't hard to convince me. It was a different kind of driving than I did in my Subaru wagon. I spent many hours driving my new truck along the coast, looking for places to walk. The truck was so comfortable, I increased my range. Something stirred in me, a love of movement for its own sake, a trace of Grandpa Ernie and Starlight. The difference was, I wasn't leaving anybody behind when I drove off.

As my treks became more complicated, I fitted the truck with some self-styled modifications. I carried water, oil, battery cables, flashlights, flares, tire fixit, washer fluid and antifreeze, a heavy-duty jack, rope, chains, toolbox with standard and metric gadgets stowed in a detachable locker secured on the truck bed. I'd always understood machines but I reached a new peak of knowledge about my truck's mechanical nature that extended to most vehicles. I learned to jolly my ride out of gullies and glide it over wet metal bridges. The scale of that small truck was perfect, I felt at home behind the wheel. I had another locker built to hold camping gear (tent, sleeping bag, first aid kit, waxed fire bricks, many matches and lighters, tea candles, dry clothes, ponchos, lots of socks (that doubled as gloves and pot holders), plastic bottles of glucose water, pouches of trail mix, more matches and lighters). Most often I'd nap in the truck about six hours into a trip then check into a cheap-but-clean motel six hours after that. I appreciated a hot shower and sleeping stretched out in order to ease my hip. Every third day I went to a place with a pool and hot tub, it helped to exercise on the long trips.

The first time I helped somebody get their car out of a jam, I really believe I saved the lives of two little children. The parents were screaming at each other at the trunk of a car that was sunk to the back rims in a gully next to the country road I had decided to explore. The kids were beyond bored, they were wandering off the shoulder onto the road. I braked to a stop about sixty feet in front of the tots and had to honk the horn to get the couple's attention. The mother shrieked and ran for her kids, the dad sagged against the car and it settled another inch into the muck. I went to the back of my truck and got a shovel. I let him figure out that he'd never be able to get lift until he ground in more dirt around the wheels. Shoving the shovel into the ground seemed to ease his temper, <u>see</u>, he was <u>doing</u> something to help (I remember not being surprised he hadn't run to the kids). From what I gathered, she drove them into this situation under his direct, express guidance. She had not wanted to attempt a three-point turn on the narrow road, voting to continue forward in the hope of finding a turnaround. There was one, in fact, about a mile up but I don't think the husband would have made it that much farther without blowing his gasket. He was lost and blaming the maps of the world, insistent on returning to the point of divergence rather than proceeding to a new point of convergence. I let him shovel while I shared some trail mix and jug water with the family. The kids liked the jug because it gurgled. About thirty shovels later he'd firmed up the muck as best he could plus he'd ground down the gully wall a bit. We planned to lift the back end hoping the front wheel drive under the engine would be our saving grace. It probably would have worked but to my relief a car came by with a trio of fishermen who were willing to don their boots and give us a hand with the hoisting. We all squished up out of the gully, mission accomplished. I felt useful. Useful to these people, satisfied with myself.

    Over the next year I intervened another three times, careful to see if my help would be appreciated rather than idly bumbling into situations. I knew not to ask too many questions, paying attention to the mechanical difficulty that was presenting itself. Blown tire, out of gas, hung up on a stump. It didn't become a crusade or anything, sometimes it happened that I was roaming the roads and could be of help. I used to call the hardware store or its answering service so I could tell somebody where I was and what I was doing. I was wary of robbers who lure in Samaritans with a disabled vehicle. I made sure the person I was about to meet saw that I was reporting in somewhere before I even stopped my truck. I was not without appreciation of the danger in life. I admit I've driven by a few times. Thanks to the radio phone, I can call it in and let it go.

So we're playing poker one evening and Gary, the gas station owner, declares he is going to retire. The other guys talk him out of that, what would he do all day? Card games didn't start before dark. What he wants to do, they suggest, is spin off some of his duties, you know, "dis-incorporate". Like, for instance, the towing and road assistance. He was always telling us he was tired of that, he liked sitting in the shop watching the pumps earn him money, selling snacks, chatting with the people. Towing was for the young. Even as we laughingly resumed the game, I got a glimmer of an idea.

I wanted to work a tow truck. I wanted to make it my business to unjam vehicles and save the people. And make a living.

I had enough in the bank to buy the tow business outright but why do that? Gary was willing to co-own it with me for the first three years and take his portion off the top. That gave me some breathing room and kept the extent of my financial holdings private. I banked locally in the usual small amounts, each quarter I'd plop a deposit from my big fund into my sea shore account. It was my intention to make towing a paying business in thirty-six months, having to finance the truck separate from the "goodwill" of remaining associated with the town's better gas station. On the other hand, I didn't want to work too hard so I hired on-call helpers. Some of the jobs were easy enough but I didn't want to strain my hip crawling under stuck trucks. I intended to succeed with science (leverage, momentum), logic, reliability, and help.

My first official call for the truck after I bought the business involved the Belzinger twins. These two aged women darted about in a Volkswagen microbus that was forever breaking down. Since they never left the confines of town, they weren't worried about being stranded anywhere dangerous. They'd just holler out to passers-by to send for a tow. Their neighbor did what he could to keep the VW going but things slipped out of alignment because the old gals drove like maniacs. They were in and out of ditches, lurching over parking curbs, or smacking into the padded stop their nephew had put against their barn (which had grown bigger and thicker over time). I had met them socially over the years at town fairs and charity functions but doing business with them was another story. They refused to believe the way costs had shot up since they'd moved to town to retire, and every dollar was stretched as far as it could go. They would barter down prices with baked goods, since they couldn't possibly eat all the stuff that popped out of their oven. (Mostly, they drove around getting baking supplies.) The Belzinger sisters were wonderful cooks and I suggested they start sharing casseroles with me because I surely should not live on cake alone. I spread the word and others began ordering from them. This put them in business for real because they could make up batches of tuna casserole, beef and noodle pie, vegetable stew, red sauce to sell in 2-4-8 portions perfect over pasta, chicken, and vegetables. I found the sisters a good quality deep freeze at a bargain price and hauled it free so they could cook ahead for a few days and freeze the pre-packed rations. I still had to haul the VW up out of various low-spots in town but they paid full price just as I had to do to stick a fork in one of their delicious casseroles. The Belzingers had moved beyond barter and were loving the cash-based business. We set up their books so they tracked supplies and equipment and cash flow. For helping them with that, I got real all-the-fixins Sunday dinners. College pays off.

Starlight was flitting around New Mexico, looking high and low for Peace and Becoming. Her years of drug and alcohol abuse had done little permanent physical damage because, she said, it was all done with a pure heart and open mind (empty head?). Nonetheless, her regrets choked her life force so she was going to the deserted desert to holler out her apologies to the universe. As I said before, she told me of her need for atonement but I couldn't imagine how she planned to give a little boy back his "mommy" – that place in my heart was filled with my grandmother. From a mature perspective, I was glad Starlight had stopped her wild lifestyle if only to reduce the risk she'd hurt somebody else. Somehow she gained possession of a Dodge Dart so at least she wasn't hitchhiking any more. She clocked in on driving citations as a habitual speeder and I could imagine her chattering to herself behind the wheel, head full of visions. We didn't spend a lot of time together (there was no model for it), she would come to town to visit but I'd only take a walk and have dinner with her before she hit the road again. No moss on that old stone, as if a little green on her north face would taint her burned-hard surface. She'd absorbed much too much sunshine and her skin was leathery. It made her look tough but she was really a dandelion seed at the mercy of breezes, a hard brown pellet under white fluffy dreams that set her aloft.

 I believe in tradition and duty, I understand my Grandfather Carl's caution in dealing with me. I had been a foundling dropped in their garden and he knew he would have to adjust to my presence in his home day and night *for decades*. He didn't begrudge me that but it wasn't free. I was to learn how concrete the role of caretaker could be. My grandmother filled my days and nights with acceptance, coziness, conversation. She arranged for me to play with other kids since I had no siblings upon whom to practice peer interaction. My grandparents would not march up to me and snatch a beloved truck from me, like kids do to each other. The first time that happened at my play school I was absolutely amazed that somebody INTERFERED with me. I was disciplined at home, of course, but if I was doing nothing wrong I was allowed to continue doing it until I was done. I wasn't done with the toy but, still, it had been taken away. Wow. I got the idea of competition from those play groups. I met up with beings who wanted what I wanted and would fight me for it. For real. They would fight me... and I learned I would fight back. I was not aggressive but I could be provoked by unfairness. If anything, I was generous so it made me doubly mad when people took advantage of me or, worse, of others.

 Right about the time I took up towing, I got into a groove with a local woman who, like me, was tinkering with the idea of a business (while living off her investments after a divorce). Neither of us had enough to retire but we could regroup. Her idea was a Shore Chores agency. She'd find somebody to do what you needed done, she would interview them in her office before setting up the time for the chore. The workers met at the office then were driven to the location and closely led in their work by the Chore Master. She extended her services to three small towns and had correctly priced it so that her people were kept busy. She didn't do "emergencies" because once she was called to clean up after an accidental shooting. She immediately found a specialty crew from out of town and subcontracted the job, losing some money but learning a lesson (forget the "biologicals"). Her name is Sarah but everybody calls her Reed. We would go out to dinner and stroll, no matter the weather. Then we'd go to her house where we'd listen to music and, once in a while, make love. Mostly, we snuggled and mixed our bodies together using our faces, our hands; we were being conservative, figuring we had only so much time together before we faced our basic incompatibility. I loved to feel her long wavy hair slip through my fingers as I moved to cradle her skull in my palms; its rippling became the definition of her femininity. In some ways we were old-fashioned about sex, not discussing it in clinical terms. Neither of us offered up much detail about our romantic pasts. We were both available at the moment for a moment.

    Reed thought I was cynical which would be true, in the sense I'm a doubter and a tester. I contend it is possible to be optimistic that the required skeptical questioning will result in positive answers. The fact is, I am a responsible person and that's key in love. My true lover would know not to dismiss me as a mere cynic. She'd see it was an effort to protect myself while admitting new information into my life. I thought Reed put too much emphasis on our romantic paths, I got the impression she thought she was straightening me out for some sisterwoman's future benefit, molding me into an acceptable escort. (Men filled the need for seed and feed.) I admit that the reason we dated formally was so we had to dress up and make conversation, we walked arm in arm and shared the evening, signifying social interaction. Neither of us pretended we were headed for the altar together.

The tow business meant I was also coming acquainted with the hot-rod crowd, which is what I called the local teens who had cars, the term was quaint enough for them to consider me cool (they presumed only they saw the sex pun since I was too old to get it, get it?). I'd be strapping a steaming Chevy in a ditch, surrounded by mortified-covered-in-bravado high schoolers, reassuring them I heard tell of these sudden gusts of gravity from the Belzinger twins... I knew these kids, their parents, their teachers, their siblings. I'd never made it a secret that I open my logs to the cops in order to qualify for an unofficial preference on wrecks and disasters (and insurance). The other tow guy does not share so easily and he gets the rowdier calls (cash preferred). Often I am sent to extricate a stranded couple mired in a lovers' lane. The beach police escorted underage paramours home after the car was freed or rigged to go. I remember being hungry for girl back when I was that age, and had some great memories of make-out sessions in odd locations. I didn't have my own car at the time but by then lots of girls did so I logged my back seat hours like everybody else. It helped me feel a bit more normal because by high school it was pretty clear I didn't come from an ordinary family so I clung to other rites of passage. Lots of children my age didn't lead "normal" lives with a nuclear family and it occurred to me that what people thought was normal was not (and if so many of us felt this way, then *this* was the new normal).

When you're little, you pretty much go with the flow. Whatever happens is your world. By grade school you have a basis for comparison because you meet the significant others of kids you know. I was always proud to introduce my grandparents and even presented Starlight as a worthy person. Still, I didn't have a dad, not even a hint of one, no picture on the mantle, no name on the birth certificate. Maybe if there had been a man around then I wouldn't have ended up being named Jeromeo Clover. Starlight signed the birth certificate while her mother was freshening up in the family lounge after her stint as birthing coach. According to legend, the name Jeromeo "came to her" as my mother lifted the pen to write my name for the first time. My designated name was to have been Jeffrey

Alan Clover but, as told by Starlight, the pen would not form those letters so she closed her eyes and let the Universe identify me. Jeromeo quickly turned to Jerry but the full version was my secret official identification. It marked me: Starlight begat Jeromeo.

    I didn't suffer a lot of disappointments when I was young; I had realistic expectations. Grandpa Carl would escort me to sporting events and church functions but balked at enabling my social activities. He wouldn't drive me to birthday parties, because he wasn't going to interact with the "mommies". They fussed over him in a way that made him feel feeble, as if were a miracle a man his age could coordinate the delivery of one kid with a gift. Grandma was more in tune with the social scene and through her efforts I got to go on camping trips and hikes with more traditional families. It didn't seem odd to me that I was included as a member of my friends' families because all of my friends were welcome in my house and incorporated into our family events. For instance, Bingo was an addiction for my third-grade gang, and Carl would call the numbers for a solid hour (no more, no less) while Grandma cooked up prizes in the kitchen. I think that routine of socializing is critical to later success, to have to actually interact with your friends for long hours, to make peace with the visitor/host roles, to grant access to your home (life) and to open yourself to the lives of others.

    My boyhood bedroom had twin beds and two desks specifically so my school chums would be able to have some space when they visited. I was proud to extend them the use of my room, knowing it had all the required elements of a good place. We could talk and laugh without bothering anybody. The beds were comfortable, I had an open space along the back wall where we could set up a fort or construct a roadway. It wasn't spooky or drafty, it was safe, it was mine. Starlight had a small room next to mine so she'd always feel welcome. Carl had the study, my grandmother had the kitchen, sewing room and living/dining room plus I got the idea she controlled things in their bedroom. It was a well-constructed house and remains the standard against which I compare my own housing. Instilling these values in me was not a matter of preaching. Grandma worked through actions. She made side-trips to pick up favorite items for us, I always had sports gear in season to fit that year's version of my gawky body, Carl had to have his special slippers. I was particular about my clothes because I had to provide the illusion of solidity from a stick frame. The pediatrician reassured my grandmother that if she could pinch my butt I obviously *could* store fat, it was simply that I was extremely fuel efficient. I burned food as fast as I ate it and if not fed would suck up any stray blobs of fat in my body. She said my furnace ran hot and I'd have to feed it the best fuel on a regular basis. I drank protein shakes and took vitamins and ate faithfully by the food pyramid and still I clattered about, all straight lines. I was light and agile so I was good at basketball (except right under the net where the illusion of bulk didn't have any impact on my opponents). I was quick in the outfield and a scientific hitter in baseball. This redeemed me to the boys in my class who weren't impressed with my most excellent grades. I wasn't smooth enough to escape a little head thumping for looking so scrawny. Wrapped around those bones were strong lean muscles (which contributed to my active metabolism) and I could bop back. I would bop back. That established, I got involved in little league baseball and stayed with the sport through high school. It worked out an important part of the puzzle of my peers.

    School may have been devoted to learning to read, write and calculate but it was experienced in a group of random individuals. Kids would come and go, changing the balance in the class. A bully left our fifth grade class and we were giddy with freedom, even the teacher gave us a pep talk about our courage in dealing with a Very Angry Person. When you have a ball of fury bouncing around a room full of children you have potential for fireworks. Kids stand up to challenge, even if the best strategy turns out to be walking away. I felt the most free with sports because I could rank my utility and know that I was making a contribution. I was a good player so the coaches took care to fill in the gaps that inevitably result when you're raised by grandparents. I didn't really play catch until I was almost eight and a neighbor took pity on me. My Grandma would toss a ball to me but I needed to feel some heat in my mitt and to shoot it back;

Carl had arthritis in his shoulders so he couldn't do it. (Later, he found a pitching-net that bounced a ball back to me which really helped me drill for skill.) It was the neighbor man who taught me to turn my hand for certain catches, to be in motion before I could think too hard, to react to the sense of transit, tracking energy. I began to develop a mathematical sense of catching a ball, arcs and angles. Geometry was a gift of language to feelings I'd discovered about spheres and movement. It was too geeky to explain to the team (or the coach) although I did tell a few guys how to step into a catch because you could feel where you had to be to meet it because it was following the only path it could. I watched baseball on TV with Grandpa Carl. I'd earned this privilege by staying quiet through three pre-season games when I was eight and a half, faithfully wearing my regulation junior mitt, my authentic-copy cap and a miniature team shirt. By the time I was ten I was allowed to stand behind the couch (where I couldn't get in his way) and pantomime at-bats and pitches. I absolutely had to move around, my body went toxic if left sitting still, and by then Carl and I had established a casual disregard. He didn't care if I wanted to act out all the parts in the game, I'd wind-up for a throw to first and then signal an out with the ump. I was silent because that was the agreement. Whatever Carl actually thought of my gyrations was known only to him, it took me a while to realize he could see many of my antics in the reflection on the TV screen. He didn't mock me about it which was quite kind of him since I can only imagine how demented I must have appeared, bony limbs akimbo, crouched to steal second one minute and popping up for a fly only seconds later. Grandma took game-time as a mini-vacation because neither of her guys was going to leave the TV area until the game was over and credits ran on the post-game show. Barring rain outs, she had a good couple hours to putter about uninterrupted, dragging blinds out to wash in the summer sun, repotting her indoor garden using the outside shed. Grandpa Carl and I had laid out our snacks and beverages before the game started, we had access to the half-bath in the hall for necessary breaks, and we understood we were politely barred from the rest of the house. She was a big fan of extra innings.

I'm house-proud from living with my grandparents. They had nice things acquired through their own effort and it made them feel connected. They'd taken care to build the best nest they could. I didn't like the idea of leaky roofs or rattling windows because it meant things were loose, not secured properly. Your home should be a place of honor. I still feel that way today. I can't even imagine having a family without including a vision of a sturdy structure for our use. My mother's abdication of the custodial role in my life underscored every aspect of it. Think how often mother's care is assumed and how notable when declined (she gave away her kid? Dads toss off kids with less remark because we don't expect them to bond like a mom.). Carl kept a low profile when Starlight was around, mercifully not needing to lord his role over her. It was understood he housed her mother (his wife) and her child (his wife's grandson); he bought food, provided insurance, took us on vacations. Starlight knew Carl gave her the freedom to gallivant in peace, and for that she truly was grateful enough to keep her free love philosophy dialed down on visits. She found me funny because I was so very serious around her. I had figured out she had a magical power over me and that my grandmother could only control her to a certain degree; Starlight bore close watch. I took comfort in the fact that nobody had any plans to change my situation. I wanted to stay in that house, in that neighborhood, in that town, planted. I watched *The Wizard of Oz* with horrified eyes, giving myself a personal mythology: I feared being stranded with well-meaning but inept people (Starlight), ripped from my world and unable to return home. The few nightmares I had included trees uprooted and houses blown down, all the sensible people gone, talking to cornstalks that were answering back.

I might be painting a rather severe portrait of myself. I was able to grow up to be a beach bum because there is enough love of life pooled inside me to add meaning to each sunset and croaking frog. I'd get away from the broiling ocean, and slog alongside creeks and ponds, seeing the big bugs feast on the little bugs, learning from the tiny world that carried on in the corners of our perspective. I was glad to be alive and living free, I was prepared to engage myself with the world. I liked people well

Book I – The Lent Hand

enough as long as they stayed in their designated places. Drunks didn't belong in the supermarket, children shouldn't be at certain movies.

So I'm coming back from using my own truck to haul hay for a guy who sold rides on his horses when two roads to my left I see the bubble lights of a beach police cruiser (there's only three of them plus a utility truck in the "police fleet"). Standing up ahead on my side of the road is a guy my age. His quick glance sorted me and my pickup into the old-boy brotherhood, he waves me over. I see an ordinary stranger in a bloody shirt. As I approach I do a closer assessment. I don't think his nose looked like that when he got up this morning – it was now smashed flat and turning purple. He said his kids and wife were being tended down the road and he wanted a quick getaway from a perfectly harmless accident for which it was better that his wife claim to be driving – as if he'd let her drive! I could guess he had warrants or other problems with authority so I said, sure as shit, hop in. I drove him the long way around town so he'd think we were getting somewhere and then popped in the back road to the police/fire compound. He was busy telling me about a certain titty bar up the coast where you could milk the cow, if I knew what he meant (pure bull), when it dawned on him there were lots of people near my truck wearing navy blue. It was just his luck that the firefighters were washing the truck while the station cops were doing the weekly yard chores. I didn't much like the guy, he smelled of booze, and he disrespected his family. Let him tell his story to people who could check the facts.

I'm sure I've met other desperate people but I've learned to let most of it work itself out. I've certainly met enough women running from abusive men to play it cool in all cases. Disaster devils its victims no matter how far they run until it strikes, or it veers for another victim. One escaping battered wife made the mistake of running to her sister-in-law who lived about ten miles north of the shore – she should have picked an anonymous refuge. I had been called to pull a decrepit Mustang out of the hosts' garage so the battered wife could hide her car in there to at least delay discovery of her presence while they tried to figure out what to do. No sooner had I hooked the little Ford and driven to the end of their access lane than I spied a green something shooting up the main line, out of the corner of my eye I saw the reflection of the garage door closing behind me. I quickly jackknifed the Mustang across the road and was tossing down flares when a green vehicle took the corner on two wheels. I'd left him just enough room to swerve into the field on his side of the road. I was heavily insured and he was clearly in the wrong, so I couldn't care less if it cost him a fortune to act like an asshole. He headed for the field which decision led, sadly, to ripping off his muffler and puncturing his radiator plus it did some bad stuff to his rims. He did miss hitting the Mustang (that made things much easier for me in the long run) but kissed his steering wheel when his car bucked up out of the road ditch. Ouch. He had loose teeth in his lap when I walked over to check on him, I had already been on the phone to the cops. His intentions were evil; he was enraged at being delayed, impervious to the pain, arrogant enough to threaten to hijack my truck if I didn't unhitch the Mustang and get him back on the road. I was careful not to point out he could have walked up the access road faster than his car would ever make it, instead I thoughtfully thought about his offer and continued to play slow and stupid so he could relax and think he was dominating the situation. Lights off, sirens silent, two cruisers materialized at the end of the road. I raised my hands in a helpless gesture... I was sick of his voice blubbering out around his smashed gums; I'd seen the look on his wife's face when she thought he'd be coming after her. He was repulsive.

    I had nothing to complain about. My dating life puttered along with Reed. We were too young to be free of society's expectations to pair up so we let people tease us about getting hitched, tying the knot, shouldering the yoke. What lovely images for a life... hobbled together. To be fair, people like my grandparents <u>had</u> to be married. My grandmother required the responsibility of a mate to see herself as complete. It gave her life structure and meaning to make breakfast, lunch, dinner, and to care for a house. She made a wiser second choice for a mate when she accepted Carl, and they both fulfilled their ends of the bargain. Carl Lewiss was secure enough to respect my grandmother's own money and to take from her earnings a fair share for household expenses. He appreciated her contribution to the family budget and that pleased her because it was only a portion of what she earned. The rest, fair and square, was hers to use. She taught me to be smart about charity. She suggested the fire/police squads run a fabric drive for quilting material. Once they'd gathered up all the spare fabric in town she convinced them they could cut squares while they waited for their calls. In two months she had the material for so many quilts she had to enlist quilting volunteers and *they* had so much fun working together that they made it a twice-yearly weekend event. All the quilts went to the county pediatric ward where each patient picked out their favorite and got to take it home with them. We heard one of the little kids asked to be buried with his, so he wouldn't be chilly sleeping in his grave. I don't think any of us will ever get over that one (the pattern was Random Silver Stars on Night Sky Blue so each quilt turned out slightly different; they made it their signature design).

    I am also grateful for Carl Lewiss's lesson about sticks. When I was just a boy playing in the country yard that separated the stables from the house, he would take time out to explain to me which things to leave alone, specifically his roses and the pricker bushes he'd planted under each of the windows. For my safety and education, he'd pick up a stick and lift thorny branches, or prod a spider so I could observe its speed. I picked up the idea that a bit of distance could be a good idea when approaching new things. I turned over rocks by prying them up with a stick, I poked at things and felt good I wasn't leaving my human scent by touching them directly. I relocated a fair amount of bugs with a contrived sling/trap (which is really just a stick with a leaf pocket). It helped me keep all my fingers as I grew curious about mechanical devices and chemical concoctions. I think even in my adulthood I take a step back and observe first. Earlier, I mentioned the Quinlan boy who lost his arm to a horse bite; I heard that story when I was nine and I remember it to this day as if he'd had it flamed off by a dragon. In my mind it was story of *Beast* vs. *Boy* with the boy having to sacrifice part of himself to get free. (In fact, he was poking the horse and got nipped but wouldn't tell on himself until the arm went septic. I envisioned it had been bitten clean off. [He should have used a stick.]) The world made you pay real prices, so I took my mission to survive seriously. Things in the world had ways of protecting themselves, even fatherless boys, if they kept their eyes peeled.

What longing I lacked for my mother I put into idle daydreams about my father. I had been born in the era that contemplated test tube babies and sperm banks so at least there was a scientific explanation for not having a father-with-a-face. It was the other side of those facts (in all cases there still was one man who contributed himself to the pregnancy) that occupied my imagination. Without considering the details of who may have crossed (more than) paths with Starlight in late 1969, I knew there was a man with whom I was connected, a blood line showing a trickle with my name on it (Jeromeo Clover _____). I was a seed flung to the forest floor, landing outside the big tree's shadow so I might have a chance to grow into who I am (fate again). If anybody was to blame (credit) for the situation it was Starlight. She might have aborted me, given me away, forgotten me at a festival.... Starlight carried me through the uterine era of my life and then she wisely put me in the hands of a mothering influence as was her duty to me. That is why I honor her because it certainly was a bout of responsibility in a life of whimsy.

Like most people, I am deferential to pregnant females. It is obvious they're in a special category and, in my towing business, they have a particular vulnerability. Often they have other children to contend with; malfunctioning transportation can be a nightmare. Or not. Goldie Crowe was about seven months along when I found her car mired off the road near Ocean Creek. She was watching the clouds skip across the water, her toddler asleep in his car seat. She whispered her question: might I come back later, she was going to call for a tow in about an hour. In the meantime, it seemed life was telling her she belonged there on the creek bed. She was stunningly beautiful at the moment and I promised to wait for her summons. I drove off to the main fork and parked there, having nowhere else to go for the moment. I didn't think it was a bad idea to stay close at hand because who knew what kind of jokers were drifting through?

Book I – The Lent Hand

Predators roam the coast, fish and birds and reptiles and mammals are drawn to the edge of land masses where estuaries form, these are hot spots of life and exert a powerful influence. It's where fresh water mixes with salt, where solid liquefies. We've learned a lot about the patterns of serial rapists and thrill killers and the best lesson is they count on being unnoticed so I practice my observation skills. I make a habit of scooting over the country roads watching for the kind of creep who likes to luck into a lone female in a quiet spot. Sex-creeps prefer just enough risk to heat the blood but need odds suitably stacked in their favor (cowards). I was leery of flim-flam guys [and gals], and I cooperated in the crime watch program. Crisscrossing the area like I did, my eyes were a valuable addition to the network of observers who watched life go by. This made me feel more connected which was a comfort when I encountered strangers under duress.

So, let's say you get flagged over to provide a spare tire for a sedan sitting on a rim, tire tatters litter the road; the driver doesn't offer the keys to the trunk, and you notice a screwdriver stuck in the ignition. You explain you're going to town to fetch a replacement tire – as if it were the most normal situation in the world. You drive away slowly, just one plain old job in a plain old day. Call their location and license plates into the cops and take the long way back with a tire. I wasn't a crime fighter. I was the tow guy. I would come back with the tire, as promised… after the cops did their part.

I feared being commandeered, forced to drive against my will on errands against my nature. The risks I took meeting people on the road had to be acknowledged. It just seemed to me that I should have an ace in the hole because if I ever did tangle with a bad guy, they'd surely have tried to stack things in their favor. I've thought this stuff through, and talked about it at card games and other get-togethers that included firefighters and cops. None of them thought I was paranoid. I sometimes had to take a rider when I found a lone driver in a disabled vehicle. I couldn't very well just drive off with the vehicle and leave the owner behind on a dark and stormy night since the cab company was closed in the wee-est hours. I decided on a strategy part of which included not revealing my strategy.

I used to keep the police scanner broadcasting when I drove. I now turn it off when I've got a rider. I learned that particular lesson after hoisting an overheated Honda and heading for town with the taciturn driver. "Be On Look Out, Honda Accord 96 white, state plate 334 Kilo Charlie Delta, reported stolen 13:45 this day." We both heard it clear as a bell ringing. I kept my eyes on the road and whispered, "Ow!" Unsaid, Now what? Was the car theft his crime or was *that* done to escape from another, more serious action? I hadn't heard any bulletins of a local crime wave. I reappraised my passenger, he was about twenty-five, not prone so far to pull a weapon even under stress, I could feel him thinking out his options and felt myself being judged as to my own rationality and pragmatism. He said, "I ought to be getting out right here." I said, "OK." He tossed me a fifty and hopped down then walked briskly to the strip of shops at the truck stop. I gave him a fifteen-minute head start before calling in the car jacked onto my truck as an abandoned vehicle. I didn't mention the driver's new location because they didn't ask. He had the chance to do something stupid in my truck but he didn't. He paid me for a service. The county paid the impound charges so it was just another job to me. I gave that $50 bill to the clothing bank. That's an aspect of discretion, choices create consequences, I had to be careful. I didn't know who he was, who I'd helped slip away. [Later, I heard he'd "stolen" the car from his brother after learning the brother had lost a large chunk of their inheritance and all he had to show for it was their dead dad's battered Accord.]

Now, about the town... I won't bother to tell you its real name, its true mark on the map, because that doesn't matter to you while it matters very much to me. It could be a village in Chile, a wind-whipped hamlet in England, clinging to the coast of Finland ... it was a collection of water-weathered buildings and roads that provided permanent jobs with their seasonal need for repair. The winds scoured everything, the squalls sluiced down the dust and yet there was always a sense of grit at hand. The air was thicker than you'd expect, given the ideal of clear seashore breezes. It was thick with the smell of all that water, all that mud, those marshes. In town, you'd get swamped by the smell of human machinations but the ocean winds blew it around. The best flowers grew on the land-side of buildings, sheltered from direct confrontation with the sea, using the structure as a vertical moat from life on the literal edge.

Creatures changed at the shoreline, there aquatic life took hold and very little vegetation survived the sandy world of the beach. This wasn't seashells and tiny fishes like a gulf coast; it was a cold rough brink between two forms of life. Sand was the gritty remains of rocks pounded to death by water. I couldn't have lived beyond that brink, I was not evolved for it. Out a distance you might see whales cruising their neighborhood, at the second edge where the big creatures lived, where they could leap and crash, slicing through the water. This part of the continent wasn't tamed, there was a rip current that swallowed swimmers. Little kids were kept in the froth at the edge, the waves were tough to predict, there'd be a big surge, the water line would rise twenty or forty feet in a few minutes then lap back down. I pulled dozens of tourists out of the mud on the strip of beach at the end of the public roadway. They underestimated the effect of water <u>below</u> the sand eroding the foundation upon which they were parked. Some made bonehead decisions like putting all the passengers in then trying to drive out. There wasn't a moment to lose when your vehicle was settling, skinniest driver get in and get it going in any direction you can, then seek higher drier land until you get to pavement then don't ever do that again! People who park on beaches deserve to give me money. I've got two sets of ribbed plastic planks that taper to a thin tongue to fit under tires. If the car is getting swamped, I have to make a quick decision. I've got extremely long chains so I calculate the various lines to pavement for me. Can I get effective pull on the vehicle? Where is the tide line? How busy is the sea? When we're lucky, volunteers gather and we basically yank it out of the muck and heave it toward solid ground. If the sand is too watery for us to stand safely then the car is a goner anyway. It will settle on its axles in the mud, sucking up grit, leaking sand in around the doors. At low tide we shovel out the wheels and roll it out on my planks, the sand working deeper and deeper into the car's crevasses. Avoidable pain proves out at a premium cost.

I certainly understand the thrill of driving the shore line, I admit I've done a bit of it but it isn't something to make light of. You are involving yourself in a complex equation and, when you push tons of metal along that seam, it has an impact. I voted for the horses to wear crap catchers on the beach and for pooper scoop laws too. I don't want pooch doo on my feet, don't want horse turds roiling in the water where we wade. I don't think people make good judgments about their interaction with things around them which means not only the natural resources but the human and other beings that share their space. You see the same mentality in people who insist on feeding geese at a city lake then complain about the goose crap. Plan on pounds-poop-per-goose-per-week, especially when overfed. It's all a cycle and your involvement matters. The fragile balance of nature and humans is weighted against us in the long run. We can pollute the planet but we cannot ordain its cardinal powers. We can pretend to have controlled burns in the forest then watch the wind laugh and toss the fire beyond us; our supertankers and pipelines leak onto the world's surface rather than pooling oil deep where it belongs (locked in rock); nothing we do stops a tidal wave or delays a volcano. Our concrete may stain the surface for years but a few good tectonic shakes and the ribbons of road are sundered. One large asteroid and we're shit on a shingle, creamed.

I'm sure we're making a big mistake as regards to our relations with our host planet but those choices define our species as a natural force and may be the answer to why we disappear from history in the future.

What might save us is our love of puzzling; we are an ingenious species even if that makes us prey to all kinds of mayhem. Would a chimp think to wire <u>and</u> glue a bomb to a woman's neck because she refused to pay extortion money? Apes did not deliver the first artificial heart and aren't even working on improving it. Our lower brain, expressed as basic chemicals, twists our abilities to suit its own agenda. Spikes of aggro-juice and fear-juice and joy-juice stimulate our actions and reactions to form the patterns of our personality. We construct ourselves one act at a time.

When I was about ten, I slipped away into Lego world. I used my allowance to buy more and more of the snap-together bricks and accessories so that my structures could take on complexity. I made an aerial walkway between my police station and my jail to control prisoner movement. All of my creations featured rock solid connections. I learned to build things the Lego way, to get the idea of how to combine different sized bricks into the thing I imagined. The kits got more complicated so I had lots of optional pieces like windows and gates – although those were NOTHING compared to the kits available now. I had to construct my own version of a rocket ship and it didn't come with a miniature computer keyboard brick and a battery-powered light in the landing module. The Lego guys have gotten fancy, some are even girls. They have many sorts of tools and carts and mounts (bike, horse, jet-ski). I listened to sports radio while I built and dismantled things, sometimes striving for height, other times confining myself to solid colors (a blue building, a red vehicle, a yellow gated arch). It was a state of reverie. Mostly I listened to baseball. I did listen to football because, although I didn't play it, I was fascinated by the power in the game. Basketball came at a bad time of year for me, in the winter I had a daily self-imposed obligation to look for signs of life beneath the death on the surface. I am spooked by deep winter, by endings, by cold dark. I couldn't imagine a worse fate than wandering a frozen tundra alone… to have no inkling of anything but lifeless icy gloom. Between that daily recon for squirrel tracks, winter bushes, etc., and my homework, I didn't have much time to roll out my Lego crates until I was soothed by spring's return.

    I can remember summer evenings, alone in my room, worn out from my active day, glad to keep my hands busy, almost as if they were run by robots, making component Lego modules. I'd look down and realize I had six walls, two doors and a roof ready for assembly. I didn't specifically think of adventures for my Lego people but I did feel a sense of drama as I planned my Lego world for that day. Maybe they'd be in need of a fortress, or I'd build a tunnel between two stacks of comic books. I'd talk to myself ("if I put this hinge there…"). If baseball was on, I followed along pretty specifically, imagining the base runner tagging up at second and flying to third. [For some reason, I always envisioned football from the referee's perspective. I was never IN the action but I was very close.] I was also absorbing male-thinking. Issues of honor and accomplishment are freely discussed by sports commentators to fill time. They may not articulate their philosophy directly but they disrespected cheaters and whiners, they championed competitiveness and spoke warmly of families. They didn't shame a player for a single error but hopped on a pattern of them. I liked the commentators' deep voices and hearty laughs. I knew that Carl respected sports and that helped me see into his heart. In some ways he was like a little old woman, he wanted to be bathed and tended, his coffee had to be just so. The sheets and blankets for their bed were replaced more often than mine because he claimed he had extra-sensitive skin. He didn't approve of women in business (although sewing was suitably feminine for my Grandma to pursue). He became frustrated with Lego diagrams but would watch me assemble new kits he'd purchased for my birthday or other gift-giving events, and then he would be able to alter them. He let it be known that I'd done a good job of fitting into his household; I didn't find it all that difficult to get along with him (or anybody else). People did things you'd never understand but you better be sure to make note of them.

Now, in the tow truck, I keep a few boxes of Lego mini-sets, some coloring books and markers, tiny teddy bears to occupy kids I encountered on towing jobs (the teddy-bear faces are featureless, the kids use the markers to personalize their bear). They were agitated by the situation, alarmed into silence or zinging with the strangeness. They represented a danger around the truck, especially if I was occupied with attaching a vehicle for hauling. They couldn't be in their car, they couldn't be in my truck… the toys were held out as rewards for safe behavior, helping to busy their minds. It was my most meaningful contact with this new generation, lacking nieces and nephews I had no routine access. If you asked me for a general impression, I'd say they may talk a tough game but they are still tender and young. To them, everything "sucks" even though I don't think they envision what *that* really means, to them it means bad-yuck-lame.

Book I – The Lent Hand

I'm in mind of a young girl, maybe eleven, protective of her mother. She told me they were recently divorced and having a hard time concentrating. They'd skidded into the runoff ditch when a tire blew. I would have to get the little car level before I could change the tire so it was going to be a while; I told myself to talk to Gus about slipping some good tires onto that old dog of a car. This young girl took her mother's hand and led her down the road to the gas station just visible on the horizon. They would be of no help to me at the scene, not even as company, because the girl was kept busy herding her mother along. Too bad the girl wasn't old enough to drive, they'd have been in better hands. The mother was washed out, disinterested in life. I didn't know what she'd been like before the divorce but at this point I couldn't credit her with her daughter's maturity unless it was hot-house grown by the woman's timidity. This girl was the sort I liked when I was her age; she was dignified and responsible. I doubted she shrieked with dismissive cruelty towards other kids, she wouldn't gang up on anybody. What I couldn't forget was the pang I felt when I realized that I was seeing what my own role would have been if Starlight had kept me with her. I would have been the one to keep track of the food and put myself to bed.

I liked setting up the tows, deciding whether to use the sling or the bar, how to use the ground to my advantage. I was not always right and got myself jammed a few times but it wasn't anything I couldn't handle. I did call for assistance when I needed it, I knew semi-haulers and bike-wreckers (I could sling the cycles but preferred to limit my contact with most of the riders who were either yuppies on machines they owned but didn't love or bikers who loved their bike beyond reason). Most of the calls were routine car trouble: out of gas, out of water, out of luck.

The romance with Reed wasn't going well, we'd soaked in our physical affection for over a year but it was barren (emotionally), we were too similar to mesh properly, our overlaps rubbed and the gaps were double-deep. Reed announced that we were wasting our time, I couldn't argue with that. It had been good for us to have things to do, dinner dates and a companion for the fireworks on the 4th of July. It was college roommates all over again, thrown together by greater forces but living through it individually. Reed was still physically attractive/attracted to me – we agreed we'd be fantasy material for each other long into the future. There were little strings to be yanked as we pulled free. I missed the illusion of closeness but, in fact, there was relief and curiosity in its place. I was experiencing a settling in my soul, as if were taking on weight. I was thirty years old, I was healthy, I was solvent. Whew. So far, so good.

Carl Lewiss died unexpectedly, blowing a huge cerebral aneurysm while napping in front of the TV. Grandma was working in the sewing room when she felt angel lips brush the nape of her neck. She ran to the living room and knew he was gone; she called 911 and they pounded on his corpse for a while but nothing thumped back. His spirit had fled. Lights out. I drove to the house that night, thinking of that fussy old man, constant and enduring in my life. When the infant me came along he had been in his late forties, retired after twenty years with the Post Office, working half-time at a hardware store. By the time I was in fourth grade he owned the hardware store and it was sold only two years ago at an immense profit on his original investment. (I'm so glad he lived to see that.) Well, the store wasn't worth much beyond the value of its inventory but it sat at the corner of a city block being "reclaimed" for commerce that was critical to the "design goals" for the consortium. Grandma was a rich old lady, slowly sewing baby clothes that had become her specialty. Outfits were outrageously expensive if you bought them but were given freely at the children's clinic where patients (and their siblings) got clothing at each visit.

I helped make the funeral arrangements. Carl wanted his VA benefits as a matter of honor (rather than need) and that meant extra forms. Grandma printed out each request in wavy clear penmanship, talking about life with me. She hadn't been able to find Starlight in time for the burial but that was fine, Grandma had entrusted Carl with her only daughter's only child and Starlight had expressed gratitude for that in her own fashion. There had been no question that Carl and Starlight settled their accounts. I felt the same way because I had participated in Carl's life.

I clipped the grass along the garage wall just the way he liked it, I painted the mailbox every other year even after I left home. He and I had gotten to the point we could express a bluff affection.

We had shared a point of reference because we both loved Grandma. She fulfilled their marriage so completely that even as a boy I could see they had a healthy union. Maybe I couldn't understand it completely but I was convinced they made a bargain with each other. Courtesy and predictability reigned. Carl had bequeathed me the proceeds of an insurance policy and directed some of his money to veterans' charities but most of it stayed with Grandma because he felt she'd helped him build his life's estate (even without the land bonanza, he'd ended up in the plus column). I wanted Grandma to consider her options carefully. I was thinking of a paid companion but she surprised me by inviting a young family to join her in the house. The divorced mother would be working 7-3 as a nurse and could be home by the time the two kids got out of school; Grandma was there to get them off to school in the morning (which was the predictable part of the day). Grandma didn't charge rent but they all had substantial chores, plus it meant there was a nurse on hand. My room was for the kids, already set up for two! Their mom took Starlight's room… the house got another lease on life. Unbeknownst to that frazzled mother, my Grandma intended to deed the house to her. (I didn't need it, Starlight didn't deserve it).

Grandma knew Rose Hardeen from the children's clinic where Rose was the new charge nurse. Rose scheduled and supervised the half-dozen RNs who staffed the place plus she attended to her own clinical duties. She could have made more money at a hospital but the clinic had treated both her kids when she was down and out, and they offered her a job when she most needed one and she honestly liked the work. The clinic enjoyed increased volunteer involvement after Grandma got her troop of sewing ladies involved. With their help, the clinic got on its financial feet so they could raise Rose to a living wage. She felt her nursing education was being put to good use and the job was close to her kids' school and to the church. She didn't believe in God, she said, in the sense that he needed an address so she could visit. Church provided her a community and gave her children a sense of belonging. Grandma's house was within walking distance of the clinic on nice days, and a short hop on the bus otherwise. I had to admire these two women, reaching across the years to establish a household. Grandma soaked up the love that radiates off children, staking out her own territory by building a suite out of the master bedroom plus the guest room and bath with the addition of a kitchenette. For some reason, the kids called her Mrs. Eileen.

I came to town a bit more often after Carl died (to keep up the big chores on the house; the horses had long ago died off one by one so the barn wasn't being used for any good purpose). Before the Hardeens moved in, Grandma introduced me to a widower friend who rented me his garage apartment for a comparative pittance; I liked having my own place in town. I had my extra furniture in there plus an entertainment center. I could hang around the house until after the kids went to bed, when Grandma was in her room writing in her journal, and Rose was in need of adult male company of the platonic variety. I didn't get the feeling she was "off" men but it was not the time for romance. She was building up a savings account, her teeth were being straightened, she was putting on weight for the first time in years. Although she was thirty-two, she seemed much younger, as if marrying her husband had frozen her maturity at twenty-three and it only recently re-activated. She'd been relatively responsible as a young adult but once coupled to her beer-guzzling reckless-driving husband she found herself making no progress in life. The first baby was an accident, the second a disaster. Her ex had no intention of changing his lifestyle. When she said she wanted to go to nursing school he divorced her for being uppity. He didn't help with the kids other than coughing up the court-mandated child support in dribs and drabs, never consistently, but eventually making good. It put her finances on a rocky basis and she couldn't get money together for a decent rental deposit. That's when Grandma stepped in and offered to share her home. It was an unsentimental alliance, Grandma didn't want to live alone but she would NOT pay somebody to sit around and stare at her all day. At least this way everybody benefited, and it wasn't such a big deal that Eileen Hampton Clover Lewiss was on the twilight side of seventy, rattling around a bigger house than she needed. They had a system and it worked.

Rose liked to sing and I often wondered if that was the true draw of the church for her. She never missed a choir rehearsal or performance, unless one of the kids or Mrs. Eileen was diagnosed sick. She had a smooth voice, it rolled up and down the notes of the old hymns in a pleasing way. She was a godsend to the choir director who could count on her to learn her parts and pay attention to the musical aims of the religious choristers. No time for gossip or church intrigue. I would sit with the kids and Grandma when the choir sang at services, observing the peaceful rituals, the sermons, the sociability. Like many of my generation, I didn't think I needed the church but it surprised me to relax there all the same. The kids were being indoctrinated into an ecumenical society and this church gave them one particular belief system to explore. I'd gotten the same thing out of church as Carl Lewiss had: it made Grandma happy when we went.

Back at the beach, I found myself thinking about Starlight with more compassion than I had in the past. I watched Rose teaching her kids to fold clothes, reminding them to wash their hands before they ate, she cut apples and pears into fun shapes and froze banana-strips-interleaved-with-pudding strips… much of her time was spent taking care of them. Most of her pay went to feeding and clothing them, had she needed to pay directly for housing she would have never made it financially. Grandma took the labor that Rose would have been doing in her own house and applied it to the one they shared. Somewhere, Rose would have to be making dinner, doing the dishes, supervising chores. When Carl was alive, the household routine had been simple and unchanging, he had grown frail and grumpy (although unfailingly kind to his beloved Eileen) and they could not get around town much. With Rose driving, Grandma found it refreshing to gad about a bit. All of our lives changed.

Starlight missed all of this in order to be with her Self and to experience Life without consideration of Others. I cannot imagine what existential terror she must have felt when she realized that a child was to be born from her and nothing easy could be done to stop it. The fetus could not be distanced. Abortion was out of the question because it seemed an extreme measure of horrific consequences for two essential souls – and unnatural besides, very much against her let-it-be philosophy. The child would be born, that was a fact she had to face. Plans like laying me off on the bikers were never seriously pursued, in her heart she knew I was going to be precious to her mother. I was going to be the reward for Eileen's faith in the soul who had emerged from within her – Helen "Starlight" Clover.

 What if Starlight had kept me? She wouldn't have done what Rose did, she wouldn't have learned to earn a living let alone maintain the balance of her responsibilities to her offspring. She didn't do what her own mother did and marry before she got pregnant. Starlight threw off any sort of obligation as a natural factor of her personality, accepting it in herself thus daring others to deny it. Maybe she "should" have and maybe she "could" have but she **didn't**. She was born to be a wanderer. In one sense, she was better at it than my bio-grandpa Ernie because she faced herself honestly. Her own father had dragged out a charade of caring for his family when, in fact, he didn't actually notice them individually. They were the people who got in the way of his drinking in peace at home. It was their fault he ended up in jail for drinking at the playground, and for drinking on the docks, and for drinking in the liquor store parking lot. Maybe, the way he told it, if he'd run off he wouldn't have had to anesthetize himself with booze so, really, it wasn't his fault because they made him stay. Grandma says now she was wrong to try to hold him, but at the time she couldn't imagine a man who didn't want to have a family. As she matured she saw that, indeed, there were men such as that and in contrast there were others like Carl Lewiss who required a wife and a home to feel safe in the world. A man like Carl took it upon himself to provide creature comforts and expected his wife to have the same standards. Good towels and sturdy furniture and fresh flowers, a stocked pantry, extra hay, a well-supplied tool bench… vehicles that ran and a furnace that fired up in season. I now understand the ambivalence Carl felt at my arrival, as if the honeymoon with my Grandma was over — and the true commitment to a future was being made. I believe I gave them an added dimension, one they would have missed out on without a grandchild to share (and, yes, took away much of their privacy). It was true that Carl was not demonstrative towards me but he let my Grandma share her hopes and dreams for me, he was proud to sit next to her at my school functions and to take us to dinner on our birthdays. (A: she wanted me around) + (B: he wanted her around) = (C: he didn't mind me being around if it kept her around)

Taking a cue from a memory of Carl, I proposed a large project for the Hardeen kids. Carl had taken me aside one long ago afternoon and asked if I wanted to lay some flooring in the barn for basketball and put a rubber wall up for bouncing balls? The muddy fall and bitter winters had kept me housebound more than any of us liked and it was no different for the Hardeens now. I thought we might rejuvenate the barn for Rose's kids, expanding one part for a little girl's play zone, perhaps Caroline could help us design that section? It seemed wasteful to have the empty building on the property, it could be put to use. I wanted to preserve the front room as it was because it contained Carl's workbench and horse tack. Jared could take the windowless back wall, like I had, but we'd replace and enlarge the smooth flooring. The hoop fit in one certain place so it was an oblong half-court. I paid a guy to remove two rafters, rigging angular supports so there was a higher shooting area out from the basket. The place was built like a fortress, redundant struts and closely spaced studs, Carl's attention to detail still standing.

Jared Hardeen was eleven years old, mad at his dad, worried about his mom, protective of his little sister. Mrs. Eileen seemed OK to him, she certainly knew how to mind her own business. His family had been in shambles, he knew it. Now they were making headway. He could forget, for minutes at a time, his feelings of being trapped like when they were staying in the women's shelter, symbolized by the smell of all those little kids. For security reasons, few men had been allowed on the shelter grounds and he felt like an alien seed pod, carrying a stain of potential violence in his unavoidable maleness. It seemed a bleak reality that the world was better off when the men were kept away. That's why he was particularly interested in me. I was showing up at the house on a regular basis and pitching in with chores, I didn't bellow at anybody, I didn't build myself up by cutting someone else down. I respected my grandmother, helped make her home safe. I kept a healthy distance between me and the kids, acknowledging the boy's presence with a nod when I entered the room but not peppering him with sociability. He wasn't interested in my words, he was going to measure my actions. I did phone him once, I asked him to get the old hand-truck out of the barn and meet me at the parking strip behind the house. I dropped the back gate of my truck and he slowly approached, struggling with the empty cart, getting a handle on it. I pulled out three large crates. I had him help me load up the first one, which clattered when we moved it. So did the other two. I had him place them side by side in the barn, their clearly marked fronts on view: Lego bricks, Lego bricks, Lego stuff. I'd seen a couple thousand of those plastic building materials in Jared's room when I was changing the ceiling light fixture. In the "stuff" crate I'd thrown a dozen packets of new Lego accessories so he could have the best of both worlds: lots of my "classic" basic bricks plus modern touches like shovels and cameras. He was curious but acted blasé that I saw for the struggle it was. I told him after we finished the sports room we could add a worktable and shelves in an alcove (to avoid bouncing balls), perhaps that would be a place to use the Legos. I said I wanted to be invited, once in a while, to build fantastic things with them. His eyes were hard as marbles, here was the carrot... who was holding the stick? I said that I expected him to take over much of the yard detail work, clipping the grass around the garage just the way Carl had liked it, Jared would be in charge of the compost, responsible for sweeping the porch at least 104 times a year. I said to him, in all seriousness, that I was going to be one of the men he could trust to treat him seriously. Then I walked away. I'd talked the talk, time would tell.

What is a boy to do? He had athletic potential but when times had been bad his mother couldn't really focus on getting him to practice, or pay for his uniform and gear each season, so he'd been denied this proving ground. He did OK at school, especially when he had a stable address. He was a worrier but with cause. Jared was old enough to know his dad was being a jerk and that somehow his father had consumed some part of their mother instead of feeding her, she had not been having a great life and part of it was his dad's fault. To the extent it had been her own fault, his mother had taken steps to correct it. She preached that self-reliance was a virtue, breaking promises was a sin. As for his living situation, Mrs. Eileen didn't ask for much, didn't presume much. Mostly she sewed, which was cool, and baked old fashioned stuff that was surprisingly satisfying to eat. She never came into his room uninvited, she was patient with Caroline who, to tell the truth, was prone to spacing out. Most importantly, his mother was growing right in front of his eyes, she was more substantial and it gave him some breathing room. He was also struggling to put me in my proper place. I'd hired a crew to do the sports room for us, we spackled and painted just to get our hands dirty with the work. We drove in a few ceremonial nails, but it was faster and more productive to structure a bonus incentive so the room could be done in a three-day weekend. We anchored a long window seat in an "L" shape to the workbench I'd purchased. The bench was well constructed with deep drawers and a pegboard. Caroline rolled in six wheeled/stackable bins to which we had transferred the contents of the Lego crates. He had utility lights hung in each corner, and an overhead light with a braided pull (Mrs. Eileen helped Caroline make this). There was a pocket door to close it off when the ball court was in use. Rose was concerned that we were spending an awful lot of money for tenant improvements but Grandma hushed her, no sense wasting perfectly good space. It was Grandma's barn and if she wanted it to be put to use then it would be. Grandma rarely insisted then always prevailed.

Caroline was easy to win over, she did not mistake me for a daddy but I certainly qualified as a desirable influence. I did manly things around the house and she felt that was a good thing. I was also the one who proposed we convert Carl's den into a room for Rose so that the kids could have their own rooms. Jared would have my old room to himself. Caroline would be given Starlight's smaller room to decorate and inhabit. It would be all hers, with a solid door, and her own closet to hold the new clothes that seemed to fly out of Mrs. Eileen's wrinkled hands! Grandma didn't hesitate once I suggested it. She asked if I'd take Carl's desk and chair, and his bookcases. Of course I would, they couldn't be given away because they were still imbued with his spirit and were, as you might guess, solid classic furniture. My garage apartment had suffered a half-finished air and these pieces would be appreciated. We hadn't done anything structural to the house except build the suite upstairs yet it was evolving into a home for Rose and her children. Mrs. Eileen kept to herself for much of the evening, hand sewing usually, but she came out for a cup of Sleepy Time tea about 8:30 when the kids were winding down for the night. This way the Hardeens had their private family time and still incorporated Mrs. Eileen naturally to cap the day. This evolution to established habits occupied years of our lives. Mrs. Eileen was borne forward by the momentum of the Hardeens' recovery, their need captured her heart but she evaluated in her head that they were survivors.

Then, overnight, she seemed to be slowing down, even they could see it. I really noticed because I'd only visit every other week so the changes were more obvious. Her time was drawing to an end and I knew she hoped Starlight would visit soon. We had bi-annual visits from my mother, a variation on tithing. Without a backward glance at the road, she settled in for a few hours and then she left again, not looking back at us. Jared and Caroline didn't know what to make of her, she was older than their mother and didn't even have a job; I was her son but didn't call her Mom, what kind of name is Starlight? Grandma carefully did not mention seeing Starlight in a superstitious avoidance of giving name to her fondest hope. I knew the signs of her preoccupation, Grandma would have the old family pictures on her night table; she loved her daughter flaws and all.

Starlight thought it was righteous that Caroline took the little room since the girl lived in the house, besides, she liked that I always let her occupy my spare room in the apartment when she was in town for a whole day, I didn't keep private papers or anything else that might prove uncomfortable for her. My will was on file at the lawyer's and in my beach house, my financial statements went to my P.O. box. The town place was set up as a home away from home, I included pictures of Starlight on my family wall there. In all these years she'd not appeared with a traveling companion although her stories indicated she made man-friends here and there, kept in touch with a few people from the original commune. We were a special island in her geography, a home of sorts, and I wouldn't deny that it made me respect her a bit more. She'd kept to her philosophy, wacky as it was, for all her adult years. I hadn't been able to figure out how she survived all this time but after Carl's death I found out he had given her a generous annuity when I was born so that she'd have a monthly stipend. It was not conditioned on her leaving but I could see it enabled her to do so. Grandma knew about it and believed, like I did, that it made things safer for Starlight who was headed for the road no matter what. She wasn't pushed by poverty even if she was itinerant. Rose kept her opinion of Starlight to herself.

I liked Jared; he brought my boyhood into focus just as I felt the mantle of manhood settle on my shoulders. I was profiting from my life on the beach, my role in the shore community was being established. People got to know me as I performed various jobs as needed. I helped move furniture, hauled out cut brush, I carted junkers to the wrecking yard, delivered home improvement supplies. I was the guy with a truck (for people who didn't have their own or, in some cases, didn't want to dirty their own). I had no qualms about wear-and-tear since I considered mine a working vehicle. All the lockers were water/dust proof and easy to hose down or pull out. On the job and off, I suppose I was a highway handy man. It was perverse that calls came only when I was busy with other things, I learned to segment my tasks so I could drop everything if a call came in. If it was possible, I answered immediately. The sooner tended, the better. Most towing situations did not improve with the passage of time. There were road hazards and mechanical complications to consider.

People got nervous when they were confronted with a disabled vehicle. What to do? What to do? This wasn't planned for. (Even the infamous Belzinger twins were as surprised they needed the thirtieth tow as the first one.) Why does a hose have to blow on that day? How many nails do you drive over before you get the one angled just right for your approaching tread? Swoosh – there goes your mood.

    I remember the first summer I invited the Hardeens to a week at the beach, using the excuse that Grandma didn't like to come down alone. I set them up in a seaside house that featured a bumper pool table on the porch (I told them the house was a loaner but in fact I'd paid top dollar for an in-season rental). Jared spent hours learning his shots before he resolutely invited me to play a game. I was aware this was an outreach so I played it very cool, just two dudes using the bumpers to make shots. He was a good kid and I didn't want to do anything to scare him off. My own childhood had been so stable that I had little first-hand experience with his chaotic lifestyle. I remembered kids from my grade school that were always turning in new address cards, changing bus routes in the middle of the week, eating their free breakfasts before the rest of us got to school – I understood that this meant they left home hungry every day. Jared now had his own bed, his own room, his own ideas. To forestall Rose's concerns about their future, I asked if she'd walk the beach with me and I took her into my confidence. Grandma did not want Rose to know about the gift of the house because she feared it would make Rose uncomfortable. If Rose wanted to refuse the house, let her do so to me after Grandma was dead. In a rare lapse of empathy, Grandma wasn't giving Rose the necessary peace of mind she herself felt when her own name was put on Carl Lewiss's deed to the house. Rose sat on a massive piece of driftwood while I told her, tears spotted her face, saying to me that she could never ever thank us. I told her that being rich enough to give her an old house was one of life's pleasures. I explained the tax structure, how the insurance worked, what kind of long-term improvements were on the schedule. I said we'd maintain it while Grandma was alive and then give Rose a swing-fund so she could ease into these householder responsibilities. (I didn't tell her she would be funded for up to twenty years.) The house would be hers with no strings attached. She could sell it although we knew she wouldn't do that... her roots were going to go right through the foundation into the fire of earth, they would rise through the roof to the cool blue sky.

On that first full family beach visit, Grandma sat on a chaise lounge far above the high-tide line, she didn't take chances with the surge swamping her chair. I was there to watch the kids at the water's edge. This was a rip curl area and nobody was safe when the water was busy. It swirled around swimmers, confusing them with its push-and-pull power. Some said the only way out was to swim across the rip, to try to stay parallel to the shore while you moved away from the churning layers of water. Since several "experts" drowned over the years, it would seem that there were more factors involved. The sea might spit you out, it might not (fate revealed). It was my intention not to risk even a nibble. I stood firm on the beach rules and that was that. It was *my* world and I knew the limits. I also took the kids on nature walks. Jared didn't care for pond life but Caroline often joined me to observe "cosmosis". She especially liked to find wildflowers that she stared at intently then drew when we got home, a born conservationist. Jared would come along with us, but he would have a book to read. He had decided neither of the kids would be alone with me and I secretly applauded his good sense. Their buddy system was a product of Rose's sensibilities. The kids were partners, Caroline was not just a baby to be tended by Jared, she was an ally, another being with feelings. They were affectionate, they leaned into each other when sitting on the couch, they had shared their room equitably and I think they missed each other in a way when they got their own rooms. Here's the sort of thing I admired about Jared: when he was nine he volunteered to read the bedtime story and then never failed to do so. Rose would sit next to Caroline, rubbing her back, while Jared read aloud. At first he picked easy-reading books but as Caroline got a bit older, and his reading skills improved, the books became more complicated. He even read her the "girly" Nancy Drew series although I think he was more drawn to the stories than he admitted. He was a good brother.

That trip to the beach was the Hardeen family's first real vacation and the shore became a familiar retreat. We ate junk food, played board games, patronized the tourist attractions (mini-putted, rented pedal carriages, had our pictures taken in 1890's beachwear cutouts). Often I found myself walking away from their cottage after they were all in bed, having checked the doors and windows, feeling a deep contentment. These people were snug under their covers, waves lapping at their dreams, stars alive at the dark shore... and I was headed to my own cocoon.

Without a lady friend to occupy my erotic energies, I had decided to indulge myself in some adult videos. I was careful to avoid the worst of them, I didn't mind silly plots as long as there was an arc to follow, I was slow to warm up to this stimulation and needed to take my time. It wasn't as if I was seeing any of this for the first time but it certainly was a new perspective. One film I especially liked was a lesbian strip show, part of a Gay Pride competition, where six different women danced for a female audience. Except for the absence of men, it was a traditional tease, including bold patrons who approached the dancers to slip tips into their bras and thongs, the momentary (monetary) object of a dancer's attention. The camera was a fly on the wall, witness to inverted excitement, the audience celebrating their own bodies on stage. I didn't intrude on them by watching, my thoughts were not of taking them, it was enough to see them in their natural glory, reminding me of bodies I'd know, bodies I hoped to know. Rose.

Rose was relaxing into the daily routine of her little family. She helped Mrs. Eileen with her morning ablutions before they woke the kids, it was a chatty time for them, casual conversation helped pass the longer and longer minutes it took for Grandma to get ready for the day (this coincided with the kids becoming more self-reliant). Grandma's nightly tea-time had moved back to 9:00 p.m. because she wasn't sleeping as much (and the kids were staying up later). She and I spent one visit going over her burial arrangements; that seemed to give her comfort. She told me her preference for funeral homes and decided on the songs for her memorial service. There would be no public viewing but she left it to my discretion if Rose or the kids would want to see her one last time. She directed that she be laid out in her beaded black dress with the black lace gloves, her engagement and wedding ring set was to be given to Caroline, Jared would get Carl's carved gold band that Grandma wore on a chain around her neck. I had the heirloom china and silver, her quilts, everything was sorted according to her wishes. There were bequests for the charities she'd supported in her life, for Starlight, for Rose, and still I was getting a large chunk. I would keep those funds separate and use them for the good of children, as she had in her life.

Rose saw all of this working around her and grew in strength. She could quilt with the volunteers, she could plant a garden with every expectation of harvesting it. Just as Grandma and I had hoped, we had achieved our charitable aim with the Hardeens. Rose could mother her children, Jared could enjoy his boyhood, Caroline could recite her address with authority – she lived at a specific number on a particular street. In this light, every positive quality in Rose seemed to shine in my eyes. She had curly brown hair that she tied back during the day and let loose after her nightly bath… clean for her maiden bed. Her shower in the morning was quick in deference to the children's needs. Something about this ritual cleansing appealed to me, I found it easy to imagine Rose's thin limbs in the shower, rivulets streaming over her clavicle, swirling above her knees. Her hips were rounded from bearing two children, her breasts looked heavy in her shirts, she had rosy skin that pinked up when she was teased. She shared her heart-shaped face with the kids but they were not lucky enough to get her green eyes. Rose's eyes were the kind of under-tree green that makes you think of a deep forest, sun-shed green, earth-fed green, soul green. It had always seemed natural enough to compliment her to the children, letting them see an adult male respond to their adult female mother. I'd ask if somebody had a fresh haircut, was that a new perfume in the air? Caroline soaked this stuff up, like a princess honors the attention paid to her queen, seeing her own future. I brought Rose plants for the yard, I paid a Shore Chore crew to come up and "do" the house in the spring while she was sent off to a day spa for pampering (the crew went out to a city dinner as my tip for the extra travel). Grandma had assured me these were gentlemanly gestures much appreciated by the entire household.

As to any potential relationship with Rose, Grandma said to me, only once, that I had the ability to be the man of that house and it was up to me to decide if I had the will. It wouldn't be just Rose, it would be the kids and the property and their future history. It stretched forward to the idea of kids of our own. It was obvious Grandma thought it would be too soon to press my suit in any case. Maybe never but certainly not now. Rose wasn't broadcasting any mating signals even as she exhibited the most desirable traits of a spouse. She was taking good care of herself, providing for her children, contributing to the community through the clinic, maintaining a gracious home. She was best friends with Mrs. Eileen who filled in gaps left by her own hapless mother. I could see that mothering was not natural to all females. It was one of the species' gifts and thus not evenly distributed. Rose's potential was brought to fruit by my mother's mother, Eileen gave to Rose what her own daughter had spurned. Still, Starlight had not abandoned me to strangers, had not strangled me at birth. She'd given me life when no one else could have. She provided me the best mother she could and returned to her own mother the love of a child. Rose still kept mum about Starlight although every moment of her life she lived a different choice.

The soft sex movies were releasing my imagination; way back when I was having sex, I'd been far too involved with the detail of my lover-of-the-moment to appreciate the greater range of female traits in the world. I would stay loyal to my current partner and not fantasize of other shapes, other sizes. Now I was free to roam the feminine landscape, to envision mountainous breasts or a petite dream lover alight on my upstanding cock. I saw the passion in other cultures, other races, embodied in women I'd never meet. I was an avowed ass man and the movies did not disappoint. Something about the fundament of a female drove me mad with lust, studying her backside made me drool for the front, for the nipples and the mound, all presaged by the look of her behind. I can think of

Book I – The Lent Hand

no greater position for first admiring a female than having her face down, defined by her outline and her texture, before rolling to her back, legs bent and spread, me kneeling between them, seeing her breasts pooled on her naked torso, her arms swept up over her head, facing me, open wide open. I feared that Rose would perceive any male advances on my part as thick-headed sperm trying to get into her life; she would have taken my weight as a burden. (So, *this* is what she'd have to do to keep the house; fine, just do it and tell me when you're done.) Having lived through her divorce and on-going battles to get her ex to do the right thing, men weren't scoring high on the desirability chart. In my fantasies, I adored her, but in her presence I maintained a cool layer of impersonal appreciation.

Back at the beach I took a lot of teasing for my "family man" demonstrations, it had not gone unnoticed that I enjoyed being with the Hardeens and acted civilized in their presence. The beach people had all met my grandmother over the years and she received her share of complimentary best wishes, they praised her bravery for keeping my rogue male self in line. Rose impressed them all and it was her good quality that made them tease me so much – any decent man would recognize her worth. She had an ordinary womanhood, rock solid in her bones, predicating her choices. She joined in the camaraderie of my beach friends, if a bit shyly, encouraging her children to get to know these peculiar characters. Gary-the-gas-station guy fascinated the kids because he'd spent twenty years in the Navy and now lived at the ocean shore. They didn't appreciate the fact he'd served almost exclusively as a supply sergeant at inland warehouses. He came to his love of the ocean honestly but not from riding it. He liked the people who gathered there. Reverend Willis (his first name) took a very secular view of religious service, and was always first to volunteer for the dunking booth at the summer fair. He did magic tricks and soft-pedaled the Ten Commandments for a looser interpretation of the Golden Rule. He'd counsel people to "ask the tide" about their thorny moral dilemmas. Mrs. Dubicek ran the antique boutique and we were careful to celebrate her immigrant zeal. Her price tags would have little notes like

"Only in America" and "Lower 48 Bargain". Caroline was sure Mrs. D was a dethroned monarch from a noble but poor kingdom in Europe. Since Mrs. Dubicek established a steady stream of mechanical gadgets and other collectibles, Jared could tolerate a visit to the store for the "girls" to oooh over the 100-year old baby dresses. I engaged Mrs. Dubicek in talk so they could browse without her hovering. She liked to *sell* the items with tales of their origin, placing the customer in the chain of history that led them to living in the greatest country in the world.

My former girlfriend Reed met the Hardeens and bristled a bit around Rose. It didn't have anything to do with me. It was about sorority issues that precluded an easy alliance until the females had circled each other a few times. Reed had the hometown advantage but Rose was supported by her entourage of family. Mrs. Eileen was aware I'd dated Reed but she also knew it had amounted to nothing in the long run. I just tried to keep a low profile, assiduously fair with my attention when they were both around, never snide behind the back of one to the face of the other. I was an experienced old lion who left the lionesses to their business. I know how a pride works from watching Animal Planet with Caroline.

I was weighing the difference between Jared's having a bad dad and me having no dad. At least his existential questions were answered but those answers were hard to take: son of a selfish weak man (saved by a principled mother). He at least knew where the size of his hands and the shape of his ears came from… I could pick out a few of Starlight's features on my own face but without half the recipe it was impossible for me to feel connected to the missing chromo-donor. I was spared thinking he left me by Starlight's insistence that none of the potential fathers knew of me. I believed her because she would have told us otherwise; she let it all hang out. I thought hard about it and knew that she wasn't going to lie about something like this, my birth story had always been told in the same factual narrative as her thinking of giving me to a biker couple. I suppose she could have listed the potential men but she didn't do that. (As far as she was concerned, she told me much later, it was obvious that I was born of the world.)

Book I – The Lent Hand

My only sensible argument to find my father is to gain a genetic history but, really, that isn't the point for me. I can always get my own genetic tests done. I haven't, not yet. If I'm doomed by heredity then so be it (again with the fate). I take care of myself and hope for the best. I'm sorry that so many men are like Jared's dad, their world view takes the form of a mirror with them centered in it. He could not have *understood* his obligation to his children or he would not have abandoned them. Rose wasn't real to him so her children were wraiths. It was bad enough to experience, but Jared had to fear it was in his own bones to be that way. Without criticizing his dad, speaking mostly of dads in general, what we knew to be true was that his dad was deficient in reproductive responsibility – but his mother had a double helping. My role was also about having a man in the house in the caretaking mode, with the skills stressed in men: home repair, heavy lifting. I made sure that I contributed to conversations, that I assisted in making dinner, that I knew how to run the vacuum cleaner because Jared and Caroline both accepted me as member, in some peripheral way, of the house.

As for Rose, I was trying to keep my mind off of her, I didn't dwell on my longings for her body. If the time came, I'd know it. She was kind enough to acknowledge my masculinity and carefully reciprocated any favors so that we remained balanced. My grandmother linked us through the house, and our mutual exchanges tied us tighter each time. We shared stories because things happened, Caroline broke her toe and Grandma had a dizzy spell and Rose blistered her palm on a hot pot and I had to have a large mole taken off my shoulder. (I was left with the mark of Zorro as the surgeons zig-zagged skin over the crater they'd dug in me.) I was like an uncle to the Hardeen kids, once removed, they called me Jerry but knew my real name was Jeromeo (Jared saw my life wasn't all roses; Caroline thought it sounded romantic.).

Living two lives was doing good things to my personality. I loved life at the shore, I fit in the little town and did my duties to the collective spirit. I dropped dollars in the food drive can, paid to let the high school band wash my car, pitched in on the seasonal cleanup days. It was important to me that I stand among others and do my part. It was easy enough to leave for three or four days to visit the city, I coordinated it with the other tow guy and gave all my helpers extra pay for working "lead" on calls. I'd learned that Starlight was missing an important component of life by never settling in a truly mixed community, even as I took the taste of freedom when I could get it. I loved being in the city without a job to do, wandering downtown, never pressing forward at the curb (I knew better), at ease, in no rush, on my own schedule. If there was a barometer for personal growth, mine was steady. I was enriching myself so much without a lover that I'd felt a sharp drop-off of my sexual longings. I didn't feel broken; I'd simply turned down my pilot light. If in time I had to abandon my hope for love with Rose, I'd be seeking a woman like her: smart, capable, shapely, generous, with a taste for love. There is nothing unbecoming about sexual appetite in a female, I have heard that many women (often coupled with motherhood) become convinced that wives/mothers aren't granted intense sexual expression. If so, that reluctance might be compounded in Rose because I would not be her familiar conjugal partner. I knew she'd married her first boyfriend and I sensed she had been faithful to him. She was tactile with the kids, they all made body contact with ease, knocking hips at the sink, throwing their legs over another's lap when watching TV. There were goodnight hugs for Jared and snuggles for Caroline. Part of what I wanted with Rose was routine intimacy; I wanted to see her bare breasts in the mirror when she brushed her teeth at night. (I pictured a range of harmless ordinary scenes with Rose coincidentally naked.)

    I think of schools of fish, how they prosper when they have others like them around them, they flash in a group, seeming to know how to move along without bumping into each other – you rarely see a fish traffic jam, and mid-course collisions are uncommon (unless being preyed upon when it's every fish for itself for the survival of the species). Community fish sense the others around them and adjust accordingly. I had done that with Grandma and Carl, I was doing it with the Hardeens. I could help sling a lunch on the table after a trip to the aquarium without interfering in their mesh. The beach people were not connected like that, they were essentially solitarily occupying the same territory. They were drawn down to the shore to feed some need in themselves like mountaineers and flatlanders do. They take a spot on the Earth and call it home. I was torn between city/family life style defined by the house itself and the peace of my little cottage, the shelf I maintained for library books changing contents every other week, my clean-swept porch and a pair of Adirondack chairs with a battered pirate's chest serving as a table between them. (There were other chairs but those two were the thrones.)

One night I hooked up a Chevy 4x4 that had toppled down the only "cliff" we have in town; an unusual mound of sand popped up at the edge of town (more precisely, the town built to the edge of the mound). It was more solid than a dune because it had been formed with a mix of sand and soil. It had been fortified and a pedestrian/bike path wound around it. Some tourist thought it would be a hoot to go "off-road" and track the path. The path wasn't set for car wheel radius and he tumbled down from the 75-foot level into the scrub brush towards the bottom. I tried to right the vehicle after the medics hauled him to the county hospital. He at least had the sense to be belted-in, and the passenger cab retained its integrity. He broke a shoulder and shattered his right ankle. I couldn't get sufficient purchase while the 4x4 wallowed on the mound so I just dragged it the rest of the way down to the bottom. Taking a closer look, I called a friend with a flat-bed auto-hauler. The surface of the 4x4 looked sandblasted, there was little to salvage of the front end. The driver was insured. I'd earned my bit and shared the rest. My neighbors knew what it meant to eke out a life when you counted on seasonal jobs and tourist money to "save you" every year. Others may have had hidden pockets of fiscal security like I did, but not many. I knew enough to keep my trap shut about my assets because sharing such information leads to a different set of presumptions. I wanted to be the tow guy, a rescuer, the lent hand... I wasn't shirking my duties and that was important to me because the Hardeens were an example of a mild case of Bad Dad syndrome. Stan Hardeen had been a ne'er-do-well but was not overtly abusive (at the end he was too lazy to even yell at them). Still, he cut them off from necessary funds and was not providing for their needs. These needs were as real as milk and blankets, and his spurning that role baffled me. The kids may or may not have benefited from "quality time" with their sire but it was an absolute fact they lacked basic creature comforts when they were little. Forget luxuries. Jared didn't get a bike until he was almost nine and had a place to keep it, Caroline didn't get a doll carriage when it would have meant the most to her. That man had parked on a barstool and chose to treat his drinking buddies to another round rather than share those dollars with his family. He didn't do that once, he did that as a lifestyle. I saw versions of that in other people (mostly men but there were always a few women who'd forsaken their traditional motherhood). As long as it seemed a coherent part of their philosophy, like Starlight's life-long pursuit of intangible Worthiness, then I let it go (since I couldn't change it anyway). I didn't tolerate bullshitters and left the vicinity when they appeared.

Rose had started talking about a certain pharmaceutical delivery guy who made a weekly stop at the Clinic. Caroline was especially interested in this because she was angling for a new daddy. She had asked me several times if I would recommend some men for her mother. It had been important to establish my *neutrality*, I didn't want Rose to even have to consider whether to include me in or include me out. My role in their lives was through the house, not any particular attachment to or detachment from the Hardeens. I'd grown up in the house, it was my family's house; my beloved Grandma lived there and so did they. Jared had decided that I was probably OK but he kept up the buddy system with Caroline. He needed to fill in some gaps in his boyishness so I began to incorporate some physical activity when we were thrown together. I'd tell them it was easier to take them canoeing than drive them back to the house and return to the boathouse by myself... would they mind if we stopped off for a swim at the city pool, it was lucky their swimming gear just so happened to be in the trunk. Rose and I agreed that we'd have to talk to Jared together about the impracticality of always <u>always</u> keeping the kids in pairs. Specifically, conflicts in his soccer and his sister's ballet meant one or the other would miss too much practice if I couldn't drive them separately. He accepted after giving me a direct stare, agreeing to move one giant step toward trusting me, flashing a clear warning that he'd be watching me. Keep it up, Jared, I thought. I wasn't the only potential beast in the forest. It rattled me to get wind of Rose's infatuation with Gil, Mr. MedTekCo, a pill hauler. From what I could gather, the pharmaceutical company would collapse if he wasn't on his toes; his were the final hands that actually *delivered* the product. He was the connection. I knew he was just the right little bit taller than Rose, his company shirt seemed tailored to his solid body, he was forever smiling. He always had an animal joke to tell, he wasn't flirtatious, he was earnest and dedicated. Bemused by his kind air, Rose accepted his sweetly shy offer of coffee that led to them meeting at a PG movie, and then I was introduced to him and smelled trouble.

 Gil was looking ever so politely for a woman to land on, he hadn't quite worn out his current one but he was close; I'm not sure how I knew this but I'd met a lot of guys like him in my life. He stiffened inside the door when he saw me, reading for signs of aggression from me. My grandmother was at the stove, stirring soup stock, and this guy was trying to figure out how he'd fit in. His body language telegraphed to me that I could relax, he was just a pretty face and he would trip on his own technique. From his perspective, Rose had a good job and a nice body and, jeez, he'd gotten used to tolerating kids around, but what would he do with an eagle-eyed senior <u>and</u> her frequently visiting grown grandson? Bye, Mr. MedTekCo. Rose laughed it off, she said he was good for practice because he was inconsequential. I was charmed by her honesty and I reminded myself that women I met were making similar judgments of me. I'd learned a few things like dressing well, in specific conformance to the hoped-for standard, to clearly signal that I "got it". I knew the kind of woman I wanted would expect me to know when to tuck in my shirt and wear something other than running shorts and flip-flops. I had limitless respect for the mating dance and if feathers had been required I would have sought out a respected tribal pattern to broadcast my message. Man. Tidy. Good bargain.

It wasn't always the men behaving badly at the scene of my towing jobs. I'd met up with some witches in my time; even allowing for stress, these hags were off the scale. It didn't matter if they were made up like cover girls or bare-faced and grimy, it showed when they shriveled their lips and stuck out their jaws, it was a dry heat, they were not wheedlers. Terms were in no way uncertain. They'd insult their man, absent or present: He should have done this, not that; he was supposed to know better – then she would not be having whatever problem got me on the scene. Sniping grated on my nerves in part because I wasn't used to it. Nobody close to me had ever felt free to disrespect another person like that. If they turned it on me I stopped work and stood at attention listening, I perfected a 10-yard stare sighted out over their shoulder. They flapped their faces until they ran out of steam and then I resumed working. There was a flat fee for a hook-up. If it was a quick job, the labor was included within the hook-up charge. If it went over the 45-minute call minimum, time was charged by the quarter hour. I insisted that once the vehicle was released to me that the driver suspend all advice and theoretical insights as to fixing the problem. I was paid to take over and resolve the situation within my professional code. Injury accidents were called in to the cops, details noted even for fender benders, my logs were a public record and would be surrendered on subpoena. It was hard to tolerate the inebriated, I inventoried the car contents before leaving the scene so I noted the three beers in a six-ring holder, three empty cans on the floor. I smelled the pot, saw ring-around-the-nose on coke sniffers. I wrote down everything. (I had a checklist.) Were the headlights on, status of outboard running lights, dash lights? If it was wrecked enough to preclude inventory then I took more Polaroids. I'd gotten savvy and created Polaroid slip sheets that could be dated and initialed at the scene. They sealed onto the base of the picture acting like a wax imprint impossible to remove without leaving evidence behind. You learn by experience – some guy accused me of stealing an $1800 camera from the back seat of his overheated car. I was shocked! I had been *helping* the guy... but, in fact, I was exposed to such accusations by my own trusting nature. I figured it was cheaper to make a photo record if there were contents to protect. If possible, I had the owner remove valuables but in some cases this was not easily done. I've been accused of doing damage that was present when I pulled up the tow truck. Sure, maybe some tow guys are careless, but I'm not and I can back that up.

Jared was curious about the truck and asked Rose to ask me if he could be my junior apprentice on simple weekend calls. I told her to tell him he could ask me directly, and he finally mustered up a speech. Per our agreement, I didn't take him to any bad wrecks but he learned how to strap on the bar and lock down on the axle. He loved using the two-way radio although he never said so, he sat straighter in the seat when he was transmitting our reply to a summons. Over time, the Hardeens had come down to the shore more often, "camping" in my living room because we all agreed it was easier than renting a second house, it was more spontaneous. I'd retreat to the bedroom and Rose would stretch out with the kids in the great room. It seemed they were enjoying the feeling of having a family retreat at the shore, roughing it together; we would hire an overnight nurse to stay back at the house with Grandma and she was treated to a "spa" with manicure, pedicure, skin treatments. It was a time that Caroline could have her mother's full attention, away from the house that always needed something done, with her brother distracted by the tow truck. Mother and daughter shopped at Mrs. Dubicek's for antique doll clothes and, knowing she had buyers, Mrs. D was able to collect more for them. Rose seemed pleased that Caroline always tried to imagine who had owned the doll clothes first, when they were made, where they'd come from, and if they were from an estate sale she wanted a description of the home. It would have been easy for Caroline to turn sullen when she had been bounced around at such a young age but she kept a fresh outlook.

Rose and I would sit on the cottage porch and share a bottle of wine while the kids settled into sleep; I had upgraded the front porch with these evenings in mind. I'd torn out the old wood floor and extended it about two feet then built window-style seats jutting out from the railing, further releasing space. We helped Caroline build a candle-box with Plexiglas so the light glowed from within the protected sides. It made us proud to have her contribution affixed to the house. Jared hadn't asked me yet but I knew he had his eye on my woodpile at the house in town (what had been the country in my boyhood was now surrounded by roads and lights and traffic). He thought we should construct a wood shed. He worked on his design, incorporating plenty of air flow under a sturdy roof, as if hoping I'd get the hint from the drawings he left around. I was going to wait him out. He had to make the offer himself, which he finally did. I had a guillotine-style wood splitter that was locked down except when I was there. Jared flinched every time the wood split but he loved releasing the lever, his other hand holding the safety gate handle to prevent accidents. He especially liked that Caroline was not allowed to go near it. His maturity-factor was bolstered by these sorts of distinctions. Her willingness to let him lead the way didn't mean she had no complaints. She made sure to match his advances (if Jared could stay up until nine o'clock when he was nine, then she asserted the same privilege at the same age).

Teenagerhood was glimmering for Jared, he had more hair on his arms and legs and was gaining weight in his shoulders and calves. I'd known him almost four years and, to be honest, I was his favored contender for step dad. He knew enough about life to respect my stability. After the Gil flirtation, Rose had gone on a few dates but none of them led to a relationship. Each was a crisis in its own way, each a deliberate attempt to be a woman rather than mom/nurse. Grandma encouraged her to take her time, warning that panic led to disaster. I'd been distracted by a few dates myself but these years of comparative solitude had worked wonders on my ideas about sex. I longed for Rose with a complete appetite, to hold her and take her and free her. I judged the time right to drop a few signals but didn't know how to start – I needed a way to offer without obligating. At least Rose knew our two families had linked without any question of a sexual quid pro quo but, still, I didn't want to put her off. I wanted her to be flattered, not spooked. I hadn't been sneaking peeks or misinterpreting our time together. I wanted to open a new element, with her permission.

Rose surprised me by veering off to a "special friendship" with a female painter. They were huggy-kissy with each other, and I knew a pang of jealousy that Rose could relax to this extent with another human. I wanted to be the one who slung an arm over her shoulder, tickled her on the couch. It was a mild infatuation between them, I got the idea it was girlish, sisterish. The kids didn't react to it as a threat, but I noticed my grandmother kept a watchful eye. She wanted the best for Rose and didn't think lesbianism was the answer. I was a bit surprised to find this a topic of conversation between Grandma and me, but I understood what Grandma meant – Rose might have been playing with fire. It seemed unlikely she would take on a counter-culture lifestyle but, then again, she'd been bitterly disappointed in her marriage and its aftermath. I avoided thinking in any detail about the potential lovemaking between the two women; it would have been intrusive, invasive, prurient (in addition to the fact it would be nerve-wracking). If this was a true desire between them, it was beyond my ability to influence. I might compete against another man but what would I offer against same sex love? I was contemplating my own feelings about this when Rose broached the subject in the dim light of the porch at my cottage.

The painter was pressing for more intimacy and Rose was uncomfortable. She had been enjoying the luxury of having a best friend when the basis had shifted, and what had been a casual physicality was taking on sexual significance. Rose said she felt the tingle of being desired but she had no matching hunger. I blinked a few times while Rose explained she could imagine kissing and even caressing another woman but did not desire more than that. *Oh?* Rose said she was lonely and that the painter had tapped into her need for human contact. *Hmmm.* The children were one kind of love but it was washed with motherliness and had less to do with Rose's own desires. *Ahhh.* As the kids got older they reduced the hug & snuggle time that for so long displaced adult intimacy. *Hmmmhmm.*

It excited me that Rose was able to discuss sex so easily with me, according it the same need for explanation as other emotional exchanges. I was on the verge of saying something about my interest in her when she stood up and bid me goodnight. My mouth hung open, what was that all about?

Jared approached me the next day with a proposal to build the woodshed. I remember wondering why everything seemed to be popping at once. Of course, I said to the boy, it was a good idea. We could go over his plans and determine the quantity of our supplies. I had only one requirement, I wanted the sides of it painted with murals. I saw artistic talent in Jared but he dismissed it as babyish. He could not value his own sense of proportion and scale, like a second sight to him, his world visually absorbed and rebroadcast through his hands. He thought the murals were a fair deal to get the chance to really build something. I'd agreed he could run the table saw if he wore goggles and followed my safety rules; he could use the nail gun and power screwdriver too. I told him I'd always wanted to be a supervisor and I intended to sit on a chair and watch him work. He seemed relieved to have me as a fall-back because he took the project to heart. It was hard not to over-direct him but, in fact, he was careful with his cuts, measuring twice (Carl taught me that and I taught him). Watching him take twenty minutes to do what I could have done in five, letting my mind wander to the Rose Dilemma. How was it that I could not break through to her as a woman? She talked to me like I was an uncle-cousin-guy to her... oh, god. Of course. I was "family" by now, custom precluded romance. Was it hopeless, then? Had our chance passed?

On the other hand, if Rose was flirting with a lesbian maybe she was more confused than I knew. Certainly as time passed, her ex-husband diminished in importance. He defaulted on the support money, canceled visits, then moved out of state. Statistics speak of male abdication and our aimless boys attest to this. We've sealed off the outlets for the rites of passage to manhood, hunting is bad, soldiering is uncool, exploration is big-money techno-centered. The evolving body seeks release and we ignore that at our peril. A population needs to cull itself or it overruns its territory. Jared found building the woodshed an extension of his Lego experience, it was something to be accomplished. He looked to the shed's support system even though none of the walls had to hold up more than the lightweight roof (plus snow load, as he finally figured out with a few broad hints from me about the rare but real blizzards we knew well). It was a simple shed, he was looking forward to putting rollers on the lift-door and watching it slide into its slot under the roof. He was building the shed to last, secure that I'd hold this land as he grew up and away (he didn't know it would be his mother's property and, some day, perhaps his own). That little building was to become an anchor point in his personal history. He anticipated the day he could lean up against the weathered shed and claim it as his own construction. Caroline ordered a playhouse but working on that didn't have the impact of his standing inside the shed he built for me. I suppose for me it was like being accepted as a real guy, working on the shed with him, I was cool to a teenager. He wanted to be cool for me.

It was getting to be Grandma's last years, her eyesight was failing and she couldn't see to sew, she'd hold one of her quilts, feeling each little stitch with the smooth tips of her gnarled fingers. I knew she wanted to rest in her house, feeling the rhythms of the day move around her, it was like she was a receding star and I used to sit in the same room not sure she knew or cared. I cared. Her choices determined my life. Marrying Ernie, having Starlight, marrying Carl, raising me. I was the beneficiary of her judgment, enfolded so I could grow. It was no secret that the Hardeen kids were surrogate great-grandkids but never was this presented as a failure of mine to provide some in her lifetime… it wasn't my time; that was all. Grandma wasn't sure I was going to deliver any great-grandchildren but if I was, it was not yet. Could I ask Rose to start another family? I didn't get the feeling she was going to fall into empty-nest syndrome since her work at the Clinic pulled her into the world. She advanced herself to Clinic Director, proud of the clinic's emphasis on quality care. She didn't expand a service until it was properly functioning. The Clinic stood as an example of cost-efficient health care. Maybe it was due to the free booties, but the babies thrived, and the toddlers bounced back from their collisions with the world in their embroidered tee-shirts (the volunteers bought plain cotton shirts then had embroidery bees. Each shirt was unique, the embroiderers were careful to hand-stitch the dragons with as much beauty as the fairy dancers). The complexity of modern medicine challenged Rose to an administrative perspective that benefited from her clinical experience. She'd earned her position and it showed. But what about me? Did I want to give up any idea of fathering my own children?

 If I committed to living with the Hardeens in town, what would become of my beach house? Did I want it vacant or rented? Sold? Would I run down there to oversee the towing business or let it go? Why wonder, when it didn't look like that was the path I was going to be offered. Rose had backed off her friendship with the painter to take care of Mrs. Eileen. Grandma's life threads snapped one by one, she floated lighter in the bed. Smiles brushed over her old lady lips when Rose sang to her, her crepe-paper eyelids fluttered as if in a deep doze. I wanted her to let go, I could see it was time, and on cue Starlight crept into town, calling me from a diner to get a status report. I suggested she go to my apartment, take a shower and get over to the house. I didn't know how sharp Grandma's senses were anymore but there was no need for Starlight to bring the musk of the road into her mother's death chamber. Rather than lecturing me on the normal fluids of the human body, my mother made haste to do as I suggested. She trusted me to tell her the truth, knowing I'd stood in for her in many ways but never had I denied her prior claim on Eileen Hampton Clover Lewiss. They sat together for many hours that last night, my mother's voice rarely stopping as she talked to her mother. I knew this was <u>the</u> primary bond for my beloved Grandmother, mother-child, and the strength of that passed undiluted through to me. I joined them at the very end, my mother and I sent our scout into the future…

 The funeral card used a picture painted by Jared, somehow he'd captured the light of a dying star in a field of northern constellations. He must have sketched it right from the sky, sensing the tale of time in the star's odd light, like a bulb on the verge of failing. We insisted the print shop duplicate the deep blues that this boy used to show his acceptance of the cycle of celestial life, a purity of energy we can only hope to mimic. I wanted people to see that, indeed, my grandmother had been a guiding light, for me and for others.

Rose arranged the music for the memorial service and collected a choir of young girls to sing the sweet hymns favored by my grandmother. Mrs. Eileen's life had been lived in praise of order and harmony, and it suited all of us that these young ladies lifted their voices for her. She'd been young like them once and was now young again in her next life. Rose told me she was too sad to sing at the funeral but I was not to be surprised if she started singing to Mrs. Eileen while she planted her garden in the spring.

Starlight spent some time with Rose after the funeral, I don't know what they talked about but it was cool with Starlight if Rose got the house, it had been Carl's in the first place so she didn't want it. The fact she criss-crossed the country precluded her stopping her journey in as mundane a location as that man's house anyway. She bought a better vehicle, tossed off a wave, and hit the road. She spent some time at the graveyard before she left, shedding her tears so they wouldn't weigh her down. I had already cried – at the beauty of the girls' choir, I cried at the sounds of dirt hitting Grandma's coffin, but in my heart I knew that I'd seen a life lived fully and I was challenged to do the same.

In order to let Rose settle into her "new" house once Mrs. Eileen's will was read (including educational trusts for the kids), I developed an urgent need to conduct business at the shore. In fact, I was going to winterize the cottage and add some security to it. I had a feeling it was time to consider offering myself to Rose and I wanted to be clear of worries when I did.

Rose. I'd seen more of her fire over the years, she had grown in beauty as she rooted down. Good nutrition cleared her cloudy skin and shined her hair, she'd added back the pounds sheered off by her harrowing days as a struggling single parent evading a bad dad. Her days in the shelter were due to financial ruin rather than physical abuse. It took her ninety days to get assisted housing after snagging a job in a packing plant and in the interim she shared a table with battered wives and beaten children... she solidified her intention to go to nursing school so she could stand on her own two feet. It did not escape her that some of the time for nursing school would be stolen from her children in night classes after her day job at the plant but she felt she had shown them the low-down side of life and owed it to them to model a way up and out, forward, toward accomplishment and peace. She didn't waste any time before filing for food stamps, public utility assistance, medical coupons, taxi scrip, any benefit to ease the budget of a student nurse/working single mom. That's when Grandma met her, her last semester of nursing school; Rose did her practical training at the Clinic. She'd requested the Clinic because she already brought her two kids in for wellness visits and had attended their Parent Class and the Fashion Cents Workshop.

For her senior nursing project, Rose had proposed a new clinic program. Parents would be grouped with a life strategies specialist or financial consultant or whoever else we could get to volunteer a speech – while the teenagers did the kid care. Teens could earn a certificate as a Clinic-Trained Child Wrangler and later arrange for jobs through the message board. The clinic included boys in the training because, after all, there was plenty of work to go around. To avoid complications, all the caretaking took place in a rented storefront next to the Clinic (which stayed open until 9 p.m., the latest Rose felt teenagers should be working). The teen was responsible for staying within arms' length of the kid they were paid to tend. Space was limited to eight "pairs" (sitter and sat) and they did a brisk after-school/early evening business. The babysitters figured out quick enough to set up board games and coloring books and ENGAGE their charges which lessened the mayhem appreciably.

Now, these years later, Rose administrated services that ranged from pre-natal to geriatrics, there was a clothing bank, a consumer referral service for local merchants, and the ongoing parent respite/babysitting program. It seemed that having this job fulfilled Rose's professional nature. She was competitive and wanted "their clinic" to do well, to serve the people, and she watched that the workers were rewarded. She couldn't always come up with cash for an employee bonus but she'd wheedle car wash coupons out of a appreciative parent or arrange for lunch to be delivered on a rainy day. Grateful merchants repaid the good referral business and, if tagged for bad behavior, often made restitution for a reported problem by donating to the clinic to buy back a bit of their reputation. She'd reached a comfortable niche and I knew that someday she might move on but, for now, this was her JOB.

Relaxed as a parent, doing good work, feeling well, looking fine... Rose.

The shore community was watching, was I going to stay or go? I had cycled in then taken root, I served a function. If I left, how far would I be gone? Would I be a weekender? A seasonal? A memory? Would I be there to appreciate the next solstice and the next? Was there any other place where guys would break off a poker game to stand under that moon and feel the ocean rock the world to sleep then return to their dime and quarter bets? I didn't really want to lose that feeling, it was as if I'd found stationary nomads and accommodated the footloose part of my nature. It turns out I hadn't come to the shore after Grandma died to say good-bye after all. I was prone to be over-optimistic when I was in that old house where all things seemed possible. No, I was only kidding myself with the idea of being a city guy all the time. It would have taken me over again, the rush to work, the need to do; the pace was hypnotic. I had a respect for the cogs on that part of the wheel but did I need to stand shoulder-to-shoulder with them? No.

I got to thinking that maybe I was thinking about this all wrong. What I wanted to share with Rose was a personal closeness that might or might not lead to lovemaking, mating, breeding. It would be self-defeating to rush forward acting like a serious suitor when, in fact, first I wanted to spend time alone with her. I wanted us to dress up and go places, I didn't want a crass physicality to squander whatever chance we had for real love. It was time to walk and talk, to get past our camaraderie and try some ardor. That insight lifted a great burden from me. I wanted us to proceed, slowly. I wanted to make some changes, slowly. I wanted to get close to her, slowly. I wanted to assert my new-thinking male self, slowly. But surely.

My old girlfriend Reed had re-married, splitting her time between the Shore Chores company and a new life as part-owner of a chain of city barber shops with her husband. What impressed me was that when I saw her I knew she was married, she acted married, even when she wasn't with her spouse. Something had changed, she broadcast a different signal, she was truly wedded to her husband and if it so happened a week went by before she could get back to town, her marriage didn't falter, it wasn't a question of proximity but, rather, of two lives being lived in tandem. I could see that kind of life with Rose, incorporating the best of all our worlds. I would never be a father to Jared or Caroline but I had a strong alliance with each of them that went beyond words. *I'd been there.* I thought of my grandmother's last days in the bosom of that family, fluttering at the edges of life, free to drift away and then reel herself back in, testing her tether. The fact is, she had a beautiful death that was in accord with her steady movement through life.

Rose began to act flustered around me and I found it flattering. It killed me to see her blush, knowing the blood was running hot inside her pieces. It was time to make my move or get out of the way because Ms. Rose Hardeen was ready to bloom. She evaluated men she saw in a way she hadn't done when she was preoccupied with the kids. Now that the kids were becoming self-sufficient she could experience more of the world around her. Even if it had been her lesbian painter friend who had knocked her back into the game, she was scenting males, reacting to males. So, I asked her to go the symphony and she said maybe Caroline would like to come and I said, no, not this time, this was Spanish opera – for lovers... she blushed and something melted inside me. She said yes and something combusted right behind my eyes. (It was either a mini-stroke, or love.)

To me, Rose was like the head cheerleader in high school, somebody I admired from afar, an impossible dream. There was the air of expectation around her, as if destined for great things. I also saw the effort it took for her to be so poised. There were social strategies to becoming trusted, admired, befriended. She was not the kind of woman you'd amble over to and slap on the butt. (As to whether there'd be playful love taps in the boudoir, I dared not consider too closely how provocative it would be precisely because it was private.) Even when stitching up the torn fabric of her little family, there was nobility in her face yet there was playfulness too. It wasn't all grim by any means. Rose knew how to make ordinary things fun. She'd call for a taxi in bad weather to take them to the ice cream parlor up the road. It would be minimum fare but priceless adventure for the kids. These were their sundae drives.

Our first kiss was at the shore. I was telling her about a senior couple I'd met on the road. Their RV had overheated because the old man had underestimated the volume of water and oil required to keep that big rig rolling. His wife paced the side of the road, I couldn't tell if she was laughing or crying but her shoulders were shaking. She was one of those trim old gals; I bet there had been many a terse verbal exchange inside that "recreational" vehicle. He looked exhausted and I knew I had another victim of RV-itis. He'd bitten off more than he could chew, it was a huge piece of machinery to fight on the road, wind shoved it and curves tempted it. It consumed mass quantities of gasoline which made it doubly-stupid he hadn't watched the other fluid levels. To his credit, he'd lunged to the shoulder immediately on seeing the gauges approach redline, and mostly we waited for it to cool down so we could replenish his behemoth. I didn't mean to eavesdrop but people forget I'm there (or don't care). She said they were selling this fucking (!) thing and getting one only half the size. All they needed was a bed and a table for quick stops on their road trips. She'd rather spend the money on simple motels where they could shower, sleep on a bed, go out to eat. It wasn't any FUN to wear themselves out dragging such a big shell around. The idea of retirement had been to get free, wasn't it? Not so she could cook in a smaller kitchen. She looked at him for an answer. He practically fell to his knees in gratitude; she seemed to be saying what he'd been hoping to hear but was unable to say. The rig was too big, period. They'd get farther, faster in a luxury camper, they felt better for voicing the truth and I envied them their positive future. I loved telling these stories because Rose really listened. This time she leaned over and aligned her lips with mine, pressing lightly to sample the shape of my mouth. I was so surprised I reflexively pulled back, afraid I'd blacked out, lost time, and somehow forced her to kiss me. Her hand slipped up behind my head and pulled me back to her lips and I felt a rush of heat, she was treating me like a male. I liked it. Way better than the movies!

Our years of friendship did not erase the shyness we felt as we began dating. To our great joy, things were different, we didn't talk about the children as much, and we discussed our lives on a more existential level rather than the daily-do of it. It was while talking to Rose that I realized how much I learned from towing. It was like having access to a behavioral lab. By adding stress to a situation, people were pushed up or down a level or two. Even on routine jobs with my pickup truck, I was called upon to change the status. I was picking up, dropping off, moving or removing. Rose made the point that I had done the same with her and the children, I'd made myself useful.

As we approached the deepening physical intimacy of an adult relationship, I was plagued by erotic dreams. I had successfully shut myself off from bothersome stimuli. Surely, my body noted its readiness each morning but a simple salute sufficed. No need for full formation. Now, as if laser-aimed, my imagination had a target and I was driven to distraction by Rose's femininity. I loved the shape of her upper arms, her feet, the set of her shoulders. I felt protective around her, not because she was weak but because in her strength she was precious.

The kids were cool with it, our going to see jazz quartets and having dinner at intimate French bistros was disdained by them as grown-up social adventures requiring special costumes and moods. Count them out. They could tell by the way I was dressed that I was taking things seriously. Their mother would look beautifully serene as I helped her on with her coat (shawl, wrap) and we swept ourselves away in the air of a haunting

Book I – The Lent Hand

perfume she reserved for our dates. She bought the scent in simple bottles marked Light, and Complete. In fact, it was an unusual bouquet, it didn't hit high in the nose but, rather, back in the throat. I knew Jared had me figured as a decent guy so he was able to tease his mom about her mad social calendar and complain that her new dresses cost more than roller blades! Caroline had grown to see the sadness in her father's leaving and was now less ready to sign up for a new dad for fear of losing another one. She was used to her life, the three of them and Mrs. Eileen, me tending the house. My grandmother's death elevated Caroline to a new level of maturity. She loved Mrs. Eileen with her pure girl heart and simply missed being with her; she mentioned my Grandma every day. I, too, acknowledged Grandma's absence and it seemed as if we all got the same idea at once. Why not invite another retiree to live with the family? We'd long since established Grandma's suite as an oasis with full bath, sun porch, private entrance. The kids still needed care when Rose was at work and when she went out at night. Perhaps there was a patient they knew through the clinic? No! How about Mrs. Dubicek? We made arrangements to lease her store at the shore in exchange for a share in the household, we knew she longed for city life after thirty years assimilating a small patch at the edge of her new world, it was too small to be her whole world. She was seventy-ish, in good health and of sound mind. She thought she might continue as buyer for the store and I examined her business plan: a manager could handle the retailing while Mrs. D. explored merchandizing in a larger territory. On her travels she planned to people watch, she was going to sit at the airports and feel the energy come and go, she'd been too long alone, and when not on a buying trip she welcomed the childcare duties. It turned her into an instant great-aunt. She'd dealt with the tourists at the shore for so long, nothing surprised her. The kids were aware of her good qualities and agreed to the arrangements. Rose trusted the older woman's judgment and let her be major domo around the house, stocking groceries and amenities like the shopkeeper she was.

 This strengthened my ties to the shore community as I took to looking in on the store with a more interested eye. We'd picked a manager who had a sideline grading school papers on a contract basis. He might do the entire year's compositions for a middle school, fairly and uniformly grading them throughout the year so they reflected both teachers and pupils. He was a perfect choice for us because there were long periods of idleness in test-grading and the busy season at the shore was his down time working for schools. I understood the guy, he was making his way in the world his own way. He had a good sense of himself and put customers at ease. The prices were still set in Mrs. D's hand expressing her patriotic sentiments ($1.99 U.S. of A.) (25% Yankee Discount) (Fifty Bucks American). He could play cards, but not markedly better or worse than the rest of us.

Rose was the sweet cream on top of an old-fashioned bottle of milk, before it was homogenized, she was the rich and vivid embodiment of a good life. I felt the same way about myself. The money helped, sure, but you ask around and you'll find not all people with money are happy. I'd tasted success defined beyond money. I liked it.

Of course, I had learned that lesson working the road. Big fancy cars driven by small-minded people; junker cars carrying a family's pride to a first year of college... I didn't prejudge anybody. I did judge them based on their actions, based on their attitude toward me and toward the situation. I didn't like being dismissed as an extension of the truck nor did I fall for overt flattery from "poor little old me" who got their vehicle stuck in the mud – this was primarily but not exclusively a female ploy. I took exception to drunks and druggies who wanted me to somehow fudge the facts; I wasn't any kinder to the uninsured. I'm not talking about towing insurance, although it is handy it does involve more paperwork. I mean, don't be on the road if you can't protect others from your mistakes. This state requires at least liability insurance so even if you have some convoluted philosophy about why you as the perfect driver do not require insurance, I don't want to hear it. Tell it to the judge. The first Polaroid I take is of the driver holding up the insurance card next to his/her license with the car license plates in the background. That gives me control of the situation. If they won't take the first picture, I'm not towing the car.

Book I – The Lent Hand

I'll call the non-bonded hauler for them, if they give me a buck for the call. If you aren't smart enough to understand why I feel I have to protect both of us this way, then I'm not motivated to do business with you. I'm called to steal cars all the time, "My car won't start outside this tavern…" (it's the ex-wife's car), "What do you mean you can't jimmy the garage door… I told you I lost my keys. Why should I have to show you a driver's license with this address on it?" (wife at husband's mistress's garage which I learned when the lovers pulled in behind my truck and boxed me in so I had to break up a cat fight and later sign an affidavit in support of mutual restraining orders as to the circumstances of my being there), "No, no, sir, I surely don't have a spare tire. Not even a donut. Nothing. Nope, we don't need to look back there. Jeez, don't you carry tires on that tow truck?" (I could smell the marijuana drying in the sun-hot trunk.). This is a shore-side community and wacky personalities consider themselves welcome.

 How many people run out of gas in a day? It must be an astounding number based on how many I see myself. It isn't only the fools who try to beat their idiot light on the gas gauge… it's mothers with children, lawyers in power suits, nuns – it's ridiculous. Every time you start the car you should check the fuel level. Don't tell me what it was the last time you looked – what is it now? The gas might have been siphoned or the tank punctured, it's only a habit if you do it every time. Think of fuel in terms of miles, I could get 100 miles, I could get 200 miles. Running out of gas puts you in dangerous situations, you don't determine where you'll sputter to a stop, pulling off to the side of any road puts you at risk of collision. You may be waylaid by highway bandits who only need a few moments to scare your wallet and laptop computer out of your hands. They're down the road laughing all the way to the next exit. Rape and murder are real possibilities since those often are crimes of opportunity. I give away clear GET GAS stickers that overlay the bottom quarter of your fuel gauge. There's no good reason to see your fuel indicator in that area. I don't like carrying fuel outside my tank so I've got a sucker-jar to transfer a few gallons into the jug. I've been offered various items of barter for gas since the person who can't keep their tank full often didn't have a lot of money. I gave more gas away than I traded for. It wasn't worth hassling. If a grown up adult person is going to tell me they don't have five dollars to pay for gas to get out of a jam then they are too close to the edge for me. OK, sometimes I've given hapless drivers cash to get more gas at the next station. I can't explain it, some people are just in trouble, they aren't making the trouble, it has swirled up around them. If my twenty bucks will get you where you have to be, then you need it more than I do. I'm most likely to do this when there are little kids or elder folks involved, every minute on the road is dangerous. I know. I clean up people's mistakes.

    The paramedics remove the bodies but they don't always get all the pieces, they leave puddles of blood and once I found a hand in a glove. We've drawn a curtain across the reality that people die in their cars, they expire twisted by the forces they've set in motion. Worse, the ones who are still alive, limbs amputated, burned, belly punctured, bones showing, screaming for somebody to make it stop. I can hear them over the groan of the lift as I remove vehicles that are already empty, I can hear them days later when I'm playing poker with the guys, some of whom may have worked the scene with me. Wear your seat belt, secure your children. Pay extra to get a shoulder harness in the center back seat. Remove hurling objects from the passenger cabin. That's what the trunk (or hatch cover) is for. I've seen the corners of heavy books stained with brains, an ice skate planted in the back of somebody's shoulder. When a car is tumbling at a high rate of speed, ordinary objects can become dangerous. Even slow collisions can cause lasting damage to occupants. I'm called to impound vehicles involved in pedestrian accidents, careful to document the damage before I hook up. People are literally knocked out of their life, I've seen empty high heels encircled by crime tape, lonesome in the road. People tossed around inside of a car suffer grave injuries, being thrown clear isn't much better. It's hard enough working the vehicles at the scene, I don't know how my medic friends take control of the bizarre situations they encounter. Impalings, beheadings, flattenings. I do my part as best I can, working to resolve the situation at least as far as it can be. I'm a guest speaker at the high school with a fifteen-minute video on accident statistics and a few spectacular crashed vehicles. In pie charts and with little tombstone graphics I show them that of each 200 students listening, so many will die within a year, so many more within two years. Look around, who will it be? You? Him? Her? (Me?) Maybe you will be one of the three quadriplegics, the lateral multiple limb loss (two arms) or maybe you're the stick figure who loses the left leg stick and right arm stick. Think about this speech when you hear of the next crash, calculate how many more tombstones accounted for in your subset of statistical probabilities. How many more to go? Still facing your chances… live or die or something in between.

    So many of these accidents are avoidable (or at least they are controllable to the extent you can reduce your damages); people freeze, react wrong, haven't prepared. Any accident involving following too closely is avoidable. Turning left into oncoming traffic is avoidable (make more right turns). Pass less. Relax. Abrupt reactions are usually not good driving. Concentrate. Put down the phone, CD, sandwich, mascara, and watch the road. Don't drink and drive. Don't drink alcohol. Don't drink coffee. Don't drink pop. Chew gum if you must but unless you're on a distance drive you should be able to do without a beverage, or else enjoy one at a stop along the way. Simple things can prevent accidents. Accidents are the outcome of multiple factors. The exact behavior that might have been successful the last time you rounded a specific curve is not successful this time because this time there is a truck jackknifed across both lanes. You have to believe that what you can't see <u>can</u> hurt you – the deer pacing at the edge of the woods is amping up for a dash! That moped is weaving dangerously. Safety devices such as anti-lock brake systems often are not operated correctly (depress brake fully and HOLD IT, the ABS will cycle the brakes for you). You pumping ABS-equipped brakes nullifies the purpose of ABS which is a self-pumper. (Please practice this [more than once] in a parking lot before you attempt to apply it on the road in an emergency situation.)

Not every road call is a disaster. Some are just witless, lights left on, keys locked inside. Except for the additional vulnerability while you await assistance, these are minor matters. The next level up is the result of deliberate mischief, maple syrup and flour in a gas tank, urine soaking the spark plugs. I've seen car bumpers chained to toilets, to trees, a yellow diamond wheeled sign welded to the car reading Cheating Creep On Board. Another had taken the ignition cylinder, leaving a note telling him he couldn't turn her on any more either. (I had to admire the creativity.) Since cars operate like portable temples, they figure prominently in people's stories. The range of car-use styles is boggling to me. People have set up sales offices, restaurants, music centers, study centers, daycare centers, kennels on wheels. Others use the floor as a trash bin collecting food wrappers and drink cups. Many cars are well-maintained but still show some personality, a stuffed animal on the back seat, a ski park tag on the rearview mirror. There are rolling caves, funky inside.

A few people have been endearing to me. A middle-aged woman from Houston was trying to get to Canada when she drove over some road debris and blew two tires. She said she was running away from home (temporarily) having left a dozen frozen homemade dinners for her husband. He was at work all day, her kids were in college, who would miss her? She had an irresistible urge to see the leaves change on Canadian trees. She couldn't talk herself out of it; she secretly confided in her mother-in-law who thought it sounded like fun and invited herself along; however, this driver declined to take a passenger. Her suitcases were in the trunk, she had an atlas on the seat beside her. (She did not have an open beverage.) She was in no hurry and took a room at the shore, the next morning she could take a shore taxi to the tire store where I would have towed her car. I mentioned there was an Oktober Fest at the city park about five blocks north of her hotel. There would be good food and cultural exhibits, might I see her there? "Why not?" she said. It seemed a pleasant way to pass the time on her road trip. She was open to life. Years later, I met her male counterpart, a professor on sabbatical, planning to read local newspapers as he criss-crossed the country. His life partner had left him; he was on his own. He needed to reconsider his transportation (this was the third roadside rescue), he was driving an out-of-shape Saab. For as many miles as he planned, I suggested he should get a reliable replacement. "Of course," he said, "why didn't I think of that?" He didn't think of it because he was intent on getting himself in motion and that car happened to be available. After almost two thousand miles he understood the vehicle's inadequacies on the road. In fact, he'd been thinking of himself behind the wheel of a Sports Utility Vehicle. No! They're hybrids and not stable. I recommended a neo-wagon, like the Mercury Sable, with the boxed-in passenger/luggage cabin, he could put a bit extra under the hood for pulling power. He needed get up and go for mountains, deserts and the flat plains in between. Solid engineering. Ready access to replacement parts and experienced mechanics. In an emergency, he could stretch out in the back. It was still suitable for city driving while SUVs lumbered through tight situations. I pointed him over to the local Internet car salesman and they ordered a two-year old Ford wagon delivered to the shore. It was a beauty at a good price and the local bank was glad to handle the fund transfer. He signed another check to the salesman for the procurement and inspection services. While waiting for the car to arrive, he'd camped at the state park. Buying the new car, he told me later, formalized his happy-go-lucky travel into serious research for a book about, well, he wasn't sure what it was about yet but he was learning something, he could read the mood of a town in its headlines. He was getting some kind of message but it wasn't coming through clearly yet, he'd have to keep going.

My own life perked along. The Hardeens had embraced Mrs. D and I thought the house must have built on blessed ground because somehow it blended generations. Rose was a sweet lover, I nestled with her in bed, enriched by the contact of our bodies and souls. The big topic was not yet on the proverbial table: The Future.

The Future was the question of children for me, before I even considered Rose's feelings I had to be sure of mine. I saw some miserable examples of families on the road, short on money, running from something, forlorn. Even those downtrodden kids had an air of possibility about them. If they survived their childhood… If they got past their parents… If they beat their apparent destiny… Was I ready to throw myself down in front of one newborn human being (or more) and claim that I would provide a world for them even beyond my own death? Years of associating with Jared and Caroline had given me an understanding of kids and I'd gotten further information from observing their friends. I hadn't spent much time around babies or toddlers but I sensed those were the richest years, they were the foundation. Nothing more or less cosmic than that. I wanted to experience the cycle of life with my own seed, yes, I could say that. How *much* did I want this became the next question. Enough to have to tell Rose that it would "matter" to me? Yes. I'm not sure it was a deal-breaker but I was owning up to liking the idea of my own offspring. She listened to me but didn't say anything back. I'd have to give her time to do what I had done and think for herself first, and then for us.

No, she decided, she did not want to bear more children. It was tempting to give me a baby (or more) but she couldn't justify it in her heart. She would possibly adopt a child, more likely foster siblings. She saw something about the world that I didn't see, she was not as hopeful as I was. It seemed in her mind that the future was not going to be a friendly place. I was surprised at her attitude given the great amount of initiative it took to run the Clinic, she surely wasn't hopeless. She said those people were already here, she could help them. She could not create a new soul to turn loose on a polluted, crowded planet. There were millions of children who needed help, the Clinic was her way of strengthening families. So I went back to my drawing board. Was it really that I wanted to breed myself into the future generations? Did I want a dab of myself in the gene pool? If so, was it vanity, then? Was I in and of myself precious to the future? (I could deposit my contribution in the sperm bank.) I decided I thought it was more important that I contribute to the survival of the race through my individual actions and less as a genetic code. Instead of adopting one child I suggested we adopt an orphanage nearby. We could find a place with a couple dozen kids, staff struggling with the finances, needing well-ness advice from an experienced nurse clinician, having plenty of projects for a handy guy like me. How many kids would be served that way? Far more than I would spawn with or without Rose.

Rose had been thinking of getting a new job, there happened to be an assistant director at the Clinic who deserved a chance to do things his way – she thought it would be fun for her, too, to do something new. By suggesting we look for a group of kids to help, in a way I was taking the easy way out… by not having kids "of my own". I think parenting is harrowing and scary (immense responsibility) and I sidestepped it. We invested in a children's home halfway between the city and the shore; it was long-term foster care for twenty kids between the ages of six and eighteen (the school years). The first project was constructing a pre-fab A-frame house for the Hardeen-Clovers at the edge of our newly purchased grounds so we didn't intrude on the house when we weren't on duty. I started leaving plans around the dayroom and posting project team sign-up sheets on the chore board. Kids could exchange household duties for building projects. I didn't have the time to develop a rapport with the kids individually, like I had with Jared and Caroline, so I went straight to the basics: I was myself and you could count on that; I'd count on you to be you. I didn't make many promises but I kept the ones I did. If I said we'd have a garden then I'd be there with a tiller and seeds. With you or without you.

The place was sitting on a good plot of land; it was run by social workers who didn't have time to come up with projects to exploit the grounds. Our garden grew with the intention of having a stall at the farmer's market during the summer. Senior kids would handle the hauling, others worked the stand. We started a dog training school that was intended to expand into a boarding operation. We'd only take four dogs at a time to simplify licensing, this project was for learning about life. The kids fenced in the runs, laid a pipe for water to the kennel. (I supervised.) Animals were important and I knew I wouldn't have to do more than put the kids and the dogs together once we had suitable quarters for the dogs. The way the kids earned time with the dogs was to walk them.

You walked your dog with other kids in pairs or trios and one staff member with a dog on a leash too. The whole idea was to create a continuity of opportunity to do and to be. We acted as a county library sub-system by having a kid committee take requests and monitor due dates on the new computer. (We also had read-aloud time in the kennels which drew the kids and pets closer. Dogs make excellent reading tutors, too, as they patiently wait while the new reader sounds out the words – it's all the same human barking as is heard by dog ears.) Once the kids realized they could check out all kinds of movies and games, in addition to books, they kept the library committee busy. We reserved the right to decline a request (especially on movies, although we negotiated a PG-13 movie night for the older kids). Still, the kids took some time to *believe* we were for real. The counseling staff had always come and gone (we slowed turnover with better pay and benefits) so we needed time to "be" with the kids. Rose had taken over two rooms for her wellness center. The kids could get skin care products, nutrition advice, exercise programs, sex education; a kid was scheduled to come in every other week, for no particular reason, but it gave excellent cover if a kid did want some private advice. She watched for signs of illness, disease, imbalance; she tracked the diabetics and took over the colostomy inspections for one little girl. Her combination of hands-on care and administrative experience made her highly effective at untangling the bureaucratic nightmare that drove the social workers insane. These kids were not available for adoption (although it was unlikely many would return to their biological families), they would live here until their emancipation at the age of eighteen. When the kids were fifteen they were expected by us to start earning their keep by taking on more complicated chores. At sixteen they would work at one of our sponsor enterprises or an outside job. We required ten work hours and allowed no more than twenty because school was the emphasis. We pioneered cooperative classes at the community college for one of our kids who wanted to be a technical draftsman, this way she got her required credits with the bonus of better technology.

The triangulating of our lives had a wonderful result, the Clover-Lewiss Hardeen household was still the center of the world but the kids' care home was an outpost. Jared and Caroline incorporated themselves like cousins would, they were just *there* doing things. Jared and Caroline still came to the shore too, maintaining identities in that small community. Caroline was Mrs. D's heir apparent for the Shore Store but first they were going on-line with her items! It would be the next generation! Caroline had the kind of soul that relaxed at the shore, she felt peace in the ocean breezes and could read the waves. Their absent father had finally gone off the deep end and landed in a court-ordered rehab program. Therapy seemed to help and he paid his support on time every month (of course, now, Rose didn't count on the money like she had to at the beginning when he wasn't willing to pay). I thought the rehab program really worked in the sense he knew he couldn't just waltz back into the family, this wasn't drunken magical thinking. He spent time with them once in a pre-planned while but the kids were primarily curious about him as an example of failure. He didn't represent any kind of hero to them. They were glad he'd straightened up and I remembered feeling the same about Starlight because I didn't want her to hurt herself or anybody else.

Caroline told Mrs. D that Mrs. Eileen had always done something for the town, what was she proposing to do? Maybe then she herself could help Mrs. D with her project like she used to help Mrs. Eileen make baby clothes for the clinic. Taken aback that she didn't have a "project", Mrs. Dubicek sat down with me one evening and told me she had hundreds of thousands of dollars in savings, beyond her retirement account and emergency funds. [That little store had been run with a smart sense of human values and so her lovely items sold quickly; swift small profits hoarded.] Perhaps she should give some to the foster home? I didn't think so. That was not her dream. Instead, I challenged her to think of what, besides money, she had to give to others. Once she knew that, she could direct her money accordingly. I had to laugh when she decided to organize, administrate and fund the town's youth baseball. She'd pay for coaches, uniforms, equipment and field costs. In return they had to have several fund raisers to share with charities in the off-season. It was to be a year-round commitment to team work, some manifested on the field, other traits developed at school and around town. She was sure that this all-American sport held the nuggets of success for certain kids, kids who maybe would grow up stronger if they allied themselves with like-minded citizens. There were three divisions, age 7-10, 11-14 and 15-18, and they often practiced together. Older kids faced their own evolution from rookie to vet. Our adult team (18+) was hardly a competitive leader in the county league but we always fielded a full roster and had people to cheer us on. We won some, lost some, played all.

Jared's best friend Eli was hit by a drunk driver and lingered in a coma for a month before his heart failed him (or let him go). Jared and Eli were only fourteen, on the verge of life, and I burned with the horror of seeing Jared's heart shatter as Eli faded away. Mrs. Eileen's dying had a rightness to it directly opposite to the unfairness of Eli's loss of life. Rose was careful to keep Jared from sinking too far, insisting they put up extra pictures of this important person, not hiding Eli's face from ourselves or our visitors. We faced this together and in truth it was a terrible blow out of the blue. As adults we were hammered with the essential fact of life: we live too fast, we die too soon. Caroline was careful around her brother, taking her cue from his behavior. Rose was the one to push him; of course, she had the strength to catch him when he fell. I had liked Eli and felt a sick anger inside when I heard how he died, I remain unreconciled to the fact that lives are lost to the selfish driving habits of others. I called the Victim's Assistance people and found out how to write a letter about the loss of Eli, each of our letters would be included as a victim impact statement after the verdict at the drunk driver's trial when it was time to evaluate sentencing. We didn't know if it would really *have* an impact on the killer but it was important that Jared commit to his feelings, leading the way for the rest of us to join him in honor of a lost boy.

Starlight was living in an ashram in Wyoming, her search for a communal life led her to that place and held her there; it was nice to know she had a cot to call her own. It might have been a small cell in a dormitory but, really, she said that's all she needed. A simple bed, a known routine, a call to travel inward. Was I all that different? I still needed to split my attention between the city and the shore. Neither balanced without the other. Rose and I had decided to have our wedding away from everybody else. It was tempting to include the kids, or even the foster kids, but in truth this was a private affair and a pledging regardless of others. It was important that we step outside the busy-ness that surrounded us. We had Jared and Caroline join us at the hotel for the second half of our honeymoon. They were an important part of our love but just as truthfully they were not central to it. This incorporated a milestone for the kids when they were trusted to fly alone (together) (first class). I loved Rose for being born Rose and growing into being Rose. She embodied what I found desirable, inside and outside.

Still, we had the "Dad" issue. The kids knew their "Dad" who had not been a father; they had me as a real presence in their lives. Calling me Jerry seemed OK. What mattered is that I went to the father-daughter breakfast and the family sports banquets. Where did the limits lie? Was marriage to their mother enough to expand the role I already occupied? (I had been the househusband.) While I had always had rights regarding safety issues meaning I could say "no", I did not have a directorial power. It hadn't been my business if Jared cleaned his room or Caroline did her homework before she watched TV but I could make them not run with scissors. There were glimmerings of maturing conflict as the kids moved forward in life. Inevitably I would have to face them as they struggled for autonomy. It helped to talk about it before the maelstrom of manhood hit Jared. He wasn't likely to pierce or tattoo himself but there seemed to be a fascination with dark games that worried Rose.

And what of the little princess, Caroline? She was good-hearted and industrious, she was prone to accidents because she was often lost in thought. She'd bring a glass of milk to her lips and somehow it would end up bouncing out of her lap. Her hip bones forever banged on corners of things as if she couldn't correctly calculate the amount of space she required. Jared was patient with her, insisting that she play catch with him no matter how often she tripped over her own feet... she crispy-dried stuff in the microwave because she wandered off while it was cooking, she'd overfilled the tub not once but twice. She was not a stupid girl but her thoughts must have been thick and sticky. I feared her kind nature would leave her vulnerable, and I understood why Jared had been so particular about backing up his baby sister. She was forever finding sympathetic aspects to monsters and villains (maybe the troll had a sickness that made him eat children, she told her brother, probably only naughty children – no, said Jared, trolls prefer the taste of the well-behaved!) It surprised her when I finally hooked up with her mother, she had removed me from consideration and it took a while for her to think that reversal through. Caroline had been such a little girl when we met that her ideas of me were firmly rooted. Still, she had a romantic prince-finds-the-princess nature, as she had always described her vision of adult love, and that explained away many of her attitudes.

Caroline got along well with adults and relatively well with her peers. Her tendency to ignore them when her thoughts took center stage had created a bit of a moat around her, she had to be reminded to pay attention to others. A circle of girlfriends had formed and they got used to calling out her name to get her attention, knowing she didn't really mean to drift away. Caroline had gotten just as firm about withdrawing when she needed to think through something. She would excuse herself from the group and sit still with her eyes closed, you could almost but not quite hear the wheels turning... it had elements of a trance. She'd snap out of it and return to the circle, head clear.

Rose had been provided a great peace of mind when Mrs. Eileen originally took over the morning routine, it was the easier set of things to do because they were predictable. The kids got up at 7:30, ate at 7:45, packed up at 8:05 and left at 8:15. If it was a non-school week day they attended the school's kid care program that featured field trips and other fun activities, same hours but more casual clothes. Mrs. Eileen would have been willing to take on the extra work of school holidays but we all decided it would be too much for her, there were weeks of vacation, and teacher-parent conference days, and planning days, so that it would have intruded more than necessary on my grandmother's routine. This morning orientation suited Mrs. Dubicek's routine when she joined the household later. Our family thrived as it was, how would it change with the wedding, which was one day, and our married life, which stretched long before us?

It is hard to resist looking over your shoulder, wondering when the bad news was going to catch up with you. I had a wonderful life, with a mate, and dear friends, security, natural beauty all around me… could it be this simple? I had to calm my fears. Was I going to question the bounty of life? In time I would see that the fact I was financially secure was more than luck, I had made choices throughout my life, I had "earned" my way, if you think of things that way. However, you didn't "earn" a bad life, did you? What is situational, what is conditional? You don't get what you deserve, you don't deserve what you get.

Book II – Family. Life.

"*Step away from the vehicle.*"
"I hate these things, Jerry."
"*You have entered the security perimeter.*"
"My own car doesn't trust me."
"*An alarm is set to engage in five, four, three, two, one. Whuuuuoooop! Whuuuuoooop! Whuuuuoooop! Whuuuuoooop!*"
"How did you set the alarm if you don't have the keys?"
"I have it pre-set to turn on when the key is out of the ignition. Maybe I should stop the pre-set."
"Think about it, Dan, having the alarm pre-set is especially important when the keys are visible inside. What you've got to stop is locking your keys in the car."
"Aw, Jerry… it's just a few times."
"You told me the car wouldn't lock from the outside with the key in the ignition."
"Oh, it won't! But, see… I take the keys out of the ignition when I open the door so the buzzer doesn't buzz, you know, if I have to get stuff organized before I actually get out of the car."
"And where do the keys go?"
"On the seat next to me."
"No, Dan. The keys go in your pocket, they clip to your collar, they hang from your belt. You need to change your routine. Or carry another key."

"My VW made me lock it from outside with the key, that worked for me."

"You sold that car twelve years ago, Danny boy… get over it."

Still love towing. It gives me something useful to do. That philosophy has guided me, strengthening me; it brought me to towing and keeps me in it. Many people don't like their jobs, they find the basic elements distasteful, wasteful or demeaning. I was too young when I left the traditional white-collar labor market to have descended into soul-killing boredom. I'm my own boss; I am the proprietor of the business, set the rules, take the risks, reap the benefits. I hire people who like to <u>do</u> things, I select good puzzlers and patient mechanics. When you've got an unfamiliar car exhibiting antisocial behavior reflecting through the driver to form a mini-movie roadside – and if you've got my rig with you – I want you to look at the situation from several angles. What is really happening? Are you towing a dead-engine or stealing a disputed asset for a jealous partner? The driver doesn't have to show you a valid driver's license (as required when they deal with the police), and you don't have to hook up the car if they don't. If the back left tire is bare of tread, what do you tell the driver about the other three? Things I've learned: mints don't cover beer breath for long, drivers of stolen cars smell hot, and too many people run out of gas.

I ask you, how hard is it to keep gas in the car? Oddly, many of the stranded tell me they were going to fill it up on their very next stop, and I wondered why they didn't act earlier, when the gauge said half-empty, quarter full? You do not need to go down to the sludge at the bottom of the tank before it is worth your time to stop at a filling station. The routine should be familiar by now, stop, pay, pick grade, pump gas, leave. Five minutes. If you don't like the smell of gas on your hands, pay for full service or buy a box of latex gloves and put one on at the station. Peel and discard. You can pump $11 or $3.55 or whatever you have… running out of gas can set off a chain of events that starts on a dark and lonely road …

"Rose, what's up with Jared?"

"Same old same old. He hates me."

"Why do you take that from him?"

"He's a teenager, Jerry. He has to rebel to get free of me."

"That's very lofty and all, but you can tell me the truth: doesn't he piss you off?"

"Oh, yes… yes, he does."

"So, why don't you stop him?"

"I have to rebel, too, you know. I can't spend all my time telling him how to live. He's got to figure that out for himself which he can't do if I'm always in the way. My caretaking days are ending for him. One reason he hates me is I'm forcing him to see that. I'm not fetching his laundry like I did when he was younger, I'm not reminding him to keep up with his homework. He makes choices and experiences the consequences."

"So all this misery is for the greater good?"

"Hoping so, honey, I'm hoping so."

My stepson Jared is coming up on seventeen, and just about my size, having stalled (in his words) at 5'10" and 175 pounds. He wants to be 6'6" and 250. Me being eye-to-eye with a brooding mass of jangled feelings isn't improving the view at home. I met Jared when he was nine, and my relationship to his fractured family back then was landlord/tenant… more precisely, grandson-of-landlady/son-of-tenant. I fell in love with his mother, Rose, and we married just a year ago. What had started as distant acquaintances because she shared a house with my grandmother became more complex as I played part-time houseman to the Clover-Lewiss & Hardeen homestead. Jared knew me pretty well but neither of us had been prepared for the territoriality that struck after I married his mom, and went back to the house I'd grown up in.

It wasn't as crude as the fact I slept with her, although that was an unspoken element. I was publicly proclaimed as his mother's man and we compromised on our living routines when I started sharing her room. I needed bathroom time, had more say in meals, deserved TV consideration and phone access… I was "in the way" as far as Jared was concerned. Why couldn't I stay in my garage apartment across town? He didn't care what went on there, and he also didn't mind when his mother and I shared the new beach house. It was having to deal with me as a member of the immediate resident family that chafed him, undercut by the realization I had first dibs since it was my family's home and he was actually the interloper. ((Doubled-back by the fact he's going to inherit the property with his sister, something I could not jab him with because he didn't know it yet.))

It was hard enough for Jared to avoid his mother, his sister, and their co-tenant, Mrs. Dubicek, let alone contend with my demands. Mrs. D had taken the upstairs suite when my grandmother died a few years ago. When Rose and I agreed to marry, we discussed our taking the upstairs as a love nest but we convinced ourselves to let Mrs. Dubicek hold on a bit longer. We spent a lot of time away from this house, down at our place on the shore or at the Kids Home we owned… Mrs. D broached the topic of her moving out but Rose quickly quelled that. Caroline was only twelve at the time, she needed the continuity of a home life during the school year. Jared could see the logic of that after Rose pointed out that without Mrs. D, he'd be the one who would be expected to "sister sit" when his mother and I were on the road. From that perspective, Mrs. D represented his freedom. I was the problem.

Much of my own teenage rebellious energy had been worn out on the farm, riding horses and fixing fences; going to school and playing in the band. Jared's generation didn't seem to have the same level of responsibility. They didn't cook, clean, do yard work, or participate in after-school activities unless you counted mall crawling. From my observation, this left them with excess vigor that soured into sullen boredom. Young couch potatoes go rancid – you gotta whip 'em up! Introduce heat or they remain raw-hard, and indigestible.

I lacked the parental authority to order Jared to take up a sport, find a hobby, get a job; commit to *something*. I knew it would be good for him but that was not a basis upon which he would rank his choices. He wouldn't take shop classes (too geeky), participate in sports (too jock), work for minimum wage (too gross). I sensed that having him invest his time in the house, which had soothed me at that age, wouldn't work for him. Jared tossed me back to my own boyhood, and I realized that Carl Lewiss had needed my help around the house yet rather than ask outright (or, even more unlikely, order me to do so), the old man let me stumble around, uneasy in my skin, lacking some element I needed to balance… he waited until I saw the answer for myself. I exchanged barn work for horse riding time. I had to go, Go, GO. I just didn't know where – so I let the horse take me. From this evolved more mature tasks to fund the purchase of my first horse, a gelded Appaloosa named Wishbone (he loved the sound of his name: "whhhh—ishhhh—böö—n*eh*"). I knew him as curious and tolerant of humans, he didn't spook around my friends. I couldn't let him have his way or he'd take off to run against the air. He loved a good headwind.

Wishbone and I were best of friends, I learned to communicate love without the easy verbal shorthand ("luv ya", "luv ya too"). Wishbone knew oats were love, clean water was love, the pasture was love, the brush was love, the rides were love. I realize lots of kids have special relationships with their animal(s) but you can't compare a twelve-pound cat to a half-ton horse. I thought about kids I knew who complained about having to use a ladle to sift cat litter while I required a shovel to handle the amount of manure my pet produced. Of course, they couldn't take Kitty for a gallop.

It was much later that I learned to love little pets due to my stepdaughter Caroline, and her deep and abiding concern for Mr. Chubby, the family feline. Mr. Chubby a/k/a Chub, Whubby, Whub a Dub, was deceptively built, he looked like he'd clock in around fifteen pounds but underneath all that hair was a bony eleven, and he brandished a bushy cracked tail. His tufted ears and toes marked him as a forest cat, good for snow, strategically shy around new things, laying low and peeking before pouncing. He'd entered our lives as a temporary houseguest then never left. He took over the window next to the fireplace, once I contrived to find a table that extended the sill… I did that after he had tumbled out of the spot half-a-dozen times. He wasn't going to give up so I gave him an assist. Caroline placed a reading chair next to the table lit with a beaded lamp she made. If Mr. C was in the mood, he'd snuggle in her lap; mostly he preferred to survey the room from his window, extending one paw to his mistress in the equivalent of a salute. He could swivel his head if something moved outside although most of the time he was content to gaze toward her, and she toward him, not staring, still communing.

Jared didn't get the animal thing. Chubby-dub ignored him and Wishbone was long gone before he arrived; he had never asked for a pet. I considered getting a house dog then gave that up in a moment of self-revelation. Any dog that joined my life was going to travel to tow sites, live part-time at the shore, work at the Kids Home, visit town. The only dog suitable for town life was the lap variety... canine miniturata. I wanted a big hard dog, an alpha attitude with neutered sex. (I couldn't have him/her leaping out the truck window and chasing trouble.) I expected dignity, presence, humor.

I met such a dog the night I got called to the scene of a big rig wreck. The driver was pinned by her right foot, the dog inside was protecting her. We had to communicate to the growling animal that we were helpers, not raiders. The driver was trying to calm him down but her voice was high and frightened, she was in great pain. I always carried a choke chain on a stick but I didn't want to poke at him when he was in the cab with the injured woman. He'd have to consent. She would have to find the strength to pull her command voice forward and reassure her dog that it was OK for me to hand her the chain, it was OK for her to put the chain over his head, it was still OK to attach the stick to the chain, it was OK, it was OK. I felt bad pinning the dog's head up against the roof of the cab but the paramedic had to get behind him (through the busted passenger window) and sting him with a mild animal muscle relaxer. (The county paramedics were cross-trained in creature tranquilization because it was a rural area full of wildlife.) Sovereign was a pit bull/golden retriever mix, large and smart and laid-back – it took this extreme situation to rile him and even then he was responding appropriately according to his breeding. He understood his leader was down, that something was bad bad wrong.

Book II – Family. Life.

Nothing like this had ever happened to him and he had never seen any of us before so these facts must have connected in his dog brain.

The hauler's license name was Magda, but she told us to call her Molly. The paramedics couldn't give her any pain relief until they could get her vital signs which they couldn't do until they got the dog out of the cab. I had been working on the problem of moving the dashboard off Molly's leg without collapsing some other piece of the wreck which put me right in the thick of the medical. I had used my Horse Command voice on Sovereign, stern and understanding, "this is what will be". I didn't cajole, I explained. "Sovereign, I'm holding your head up to help Molly. Sovereign, listen. Quiet. Now. Listen. It's OK, Sovereign, Molly is OK. Relax. Molly. Sovereign. Quiet. Molly is OK. Good boy." The big dog gradually gave over to the drug, softened and relaxed. I slid a muzzle and harness on him, careful to keep talking. I insisted we put him on a board so he didn't have to suffer the indignity of being carried in a human's arms. Molly knew things were bad, she was shocky and losing blood. I let the medical information fade into the back of my mind so I could do the math on angling a crawl space into the crushed cab. Time tumbles in situations like this, speeding and slowing, allowing the mind time to adjust. I waited for animal control to pick up the dog after the ambulance drove off with Molly; I had already relinquished the wreck to a big rig hauler. I'd been helpful in the rescue because that was small-mechanics plus I was first on the scene. Uprighting the truck and dragging it off was another dimension of power.

Sovereign wasn't happy at the animal shelter, and he couldn't visit Molly in the hospital, so I agreed he could board on our property, in a portable pen with covered dog "patio". Molly was going to be receiving in-patient rehab for several weeks then moving in with her brother and his family and their cats and hamsters while she mastered her prosthetic foot. Sovereign wasn't going to fit in there, either. We initially considered his stay a foster-family situation; however, over time, Molly understood the dog had a good life with me; he still got to hit the road, smell the country, have his own human. It was hard for me to take him from her; I couldn't have done it if Sovereign hadn't insisted. (I promised to send Molly pictures; she bravely didn't visit because we believed it would confuse the dog.)

Jared thought Sovereign was cool, admiring his power and size, and disregarding his big heart. I would have gotten another dog if Jared asked, if he included reasonable assurances that he'd be responsible for the animal's care. Jared wasn't that "together", as he put it, and so he opted for his solitary existence. Rose had song birds on the porch at the house, gifts from Mrs. D., who cared for them when Rose was on the road with me.

The family dynamics were still off pace, and it was Jared who was causing the static. I had to think of a way to discharge it, using some sort of emotional lightning rod, and I suggested the idea to put him on a budget towards earning a car. He'd get credit for school attendance, more for academic performance, extra for work around the house, and bonuses for accomplishment of pre-set goals. Drivers ed completed, $200 credit; convincing research into car price/safety ratio earned him another $250 credit. His price/safety ratio eventually determined that he would need at least $4,000 to buy into a car and insurance suitable for the road. (We would match his earned credits, although he didn't know that yet, which would increase both the cool and safety values.)

He had to have graduated from high school, and be in good standing with life, to enjoy our cooperation on car ownership. That gave him fifteen months to get his act together. Thunder rumbled after I threw down that bolt of juice, he saw only the negative, we'd be *watching* him and *judging* him; it was creepy, what he really needed was the freedom a car would give him so he could prove he was worthy to have it.

"That's cow shit, Jared."

'What?"

"Cow shit, it isn't even bull shit."

"Mom! Do you hear what he's saying to me?"

"Loud and clear. Do you?"

"What's wrong with me wanting a car?"

"Nothing, Jared. Your mother and I agree you can earn one."

"But you guys can afford one for me."

"We're affording enough vehicles to go around, when you get your license we agreed you can use the station wagon –"

" – gross!"

"Would you rather have a bicycle?"

"Grosser."

"We expect you to run errands for the family, go to school functions, stuff like that in the wagon. What you want is a private ride, your own car – and the right to disappear with it. We're not denying you've got some good reasons. The problem is your leap of making your preference our obligation. We'll work with you to earn a car by the time you're legally able to make an adult choice."

"Jerry, you can't tell me what to do."

"Your mother and I together decide what vehicles are registered at this address."

"Mom."

"Son."

"I can't believe this. How am I going to earn thousands of dollars? Do you want me to quit school, get a job… are you making me choose between soccer and working at Burgerama? Is that the life you're preparing me for, Mom?"

"Jared, take a breath. Jerry explained we will credit you a fair value for school, and that would include soccer. A kid your age is going to make about $6 an hour… we'll calculate 30 hours of school, plus homework hours, sports practice and games. That's about fifty hours or $300 a week. $1200 a month. Nine months of the school year. That's about $10,000, and that's before extra reward for good grades and community service. You pay for clothes, movies, shoes by cashing in credits… you decide how much of your credit you want to spend from your car account for stuff like that."

"Wait a minute. You're going to pay me – for going to school?"

"Credit you. We'll run an account with you. It's a good way for you to get an idea of what being on your own is going to be like."

"Yeah, like you're ever going to let me go."

"Don't kid yourself, Jared... you're sixteen. Like it or not, the castle closes when you leave high school. That's two years. By then you need a plan... college, job, trade school, Peace Corps., butcher, baker, candlestick maker."

"Now you're kicking me out; nice, Mom!"

"We want to help you prepare to leave us, to grow away... don't expect to be crashing in our basement when you're thirty."

"Most gross. And you're saying I can get a car when I can 'afford' one with this 'credit', right?"

"Yes. son. If you earn it, you can have it. It isn't just the money, you need to show us you can handle the responsibility. Driving is life and death, just ask Jerry."

Rose took the lead in our work with the Kids Place; her experience running the neighborhood clinic was a terrific lead-in to tackling social services and educational bureaucracies associated with a long-term residence facility with school age kids. Kids popped into the Place without school records, shoes, hope, a toothbrush... they needed to get into a school, any school, school can be a constant for them when chaos rules their homes. Kids don't come to us from intact families. They need physicals, dental checks, haircuts, they're entering a system.

The Kids Place didn't pretend to be a family setting that happened to house a rotation of kids. There were dorm-style lavatories, industrial carpet in the teen-style rec rooms, durable furniture, fresh paint and clean windows, a playground. We knew every kid needed their own room, even if it was small (especially if it was small and easily controlled). The Place had a poster collection for new residents to choose from, they could borrow statues, make sand paintings. Visual expression was encouraged since family violence is more vivid than words. We could never be sure who were predators and who were prey (it's the hardest lesson ((not to expect to catch all the bad ones))) so each kid got a private retreat, a safe place, an isolation place, somewhere they could run, somewhere we could put them. There were two kitchens, one up and one down, with a dumb-waiter between them (compartments too small for even a little child). There were two laundry rooms, two dining rooms. One big and one small of every place a home requires. This allowed us to mix up the groupings, seeing each child through the eyes of all the kids in one setting or another. They each had an individual dynamic but the population shifted, some Kids bouncing through, staying a year or two. Those Kids were lumped together as short-timers. It was the older Kids, the forsaken who knew they'd be there until they were eighteen and not a day longer than that, these Kids *lived* there.

Jared helped on building projects at the Kids Place. Rose and I had agreed that he and his sister could come for special activities as long as they understood that their lives were in town (the beach access was shared as off-the-clock time with family and friends from town). A new resident, Belinda, was a street kid old before her time, a tough-talking fourteen-year old child. Jared was her age, naïve like any kid raised in the middle class. He had a crush on her, which she repaid by offering to blow him if he could get them some beers. She already had plenty of acid. He was so shocked he just walked out of the room – that's what she thought of him? Later, he told me he was worried about her. Maybe the next guy wouldn't have the sense to step away. I told him there were people who analyzed situations based on entirely different perceptions than his or mine. Belinda traded her budding sex for comfort, she couldn't imagine any other reason a guy would want to spend time with a girl. Talk? Walk? What?? She eventually ran away and got herself sent to a stricter place. Jared said he thought she was so scared of her own behavior that she deliberately set herself up to get reassigned to a site with fewer choices. He sensed her fear as the fuel for her instability, and discovered that her supposed wild exterior was armor for the shaky kid inside. Toughest shells for tenderest hearts.

There were other lessons taught by the Kids. Javier was a wizard with growing things, lending his organic sense of the cycle of life to Jared's school age woes. Years started, years ended, time passed. One cycle, then another. Growing seasons, fallow seasons. Sowing, budding, fruiting, harvesting, seeding again. Javier was a homely kid, his ears were small and well-shaped but stuck out at right angles from his square head, his nose was proud and off-center. His forehead was high, his hairline was low. Javier had lived with his grandmother after his mother OD'd on cocaine, he came to us when his grandmother had a stroke. He arrived with a dozen plants in pots; tending to his collection was his lifeline to the familiar. We scrounged up bookshelves for Javier to paint the color of his choice (sand, against which his pots stood out). Flowers. Ferns. Tendrils. Ten shades of green, variations of red, yellow, blue. He gravitated out to the gardens, starting at the herbs before he lingered at the flower beds, gaining peace with each generation of color, the culling and trimming for future growth. Jared and Javier first met during the Spring Clean. Every year we started at the center of the property and worked our way outward, housework, yard work, fieldwork... we hauled off some stuff, composted some, overhauled and donated the rest. Our workshops (the main and the auxiliary) were set for woodworking, welding, wiring, assembling. Kids who didn't have any other particular interest spent a certain amount of time helping reclaim castoff items. They can be encouraged to concentrate on something outside of themselves, and measure their progress toward a goal, they could see the fruits of their labor. Javier and Jared were in the fields, sun shining its first heat of the year, they got giddy and raced each other tilling the main rows. They measured speed *and* precision which rendered near perfect conditions for growth.

Jared was leery of making friends with one of the Kids, he knew they weren't provided for his amusement, they weren't sitting ducks in his personal gallery. Guys at school bluffed that they'd be working the girls, heh heh, but Jared knew (hoped) if they saw these girls, they'd see there was no sport in exploiting them.

Caroline was slow to bond with the Kids, perhaps because she was so distant in her fondness. The fact was, Caroline never understood any of her peers, these Kids were just another subset who didn't fit the perfect equation. What we thought of as dreaminess when she was a girl turned into a well-developed sense of moods around her in her adolescence. She might not be listening to the words of others but she heard the tone. She didn't have much of an agenda so she didn't try to boss anybody around. She talked to people from time to time, when she had something to say. She couldn't be rushed even if she was generally agreeable. It was clear that Jared loomed alongside her, protectively. He trained himself from an early age to keep one eye on her and his other on everybody else.

Rose was able to steer her own children through some of the rockier parts of interacting with aching Kids. There was sadness, anger, guilt, fear, numbness. Somebody had to stand up against the furies in the Kids' lives, she held out the beacon for them to follow. She helped them to hang on, to wait out red-tape delays by strengthening themselves for whatever outcome; she had to acknowledge the disposition of a Kid's case might have nothing to do with the desires of the Kid (or her). She had to send them off, up the chain, down the river, back into the world, because their name was on one side of a line or the other in a ledger downtown. As long as they were with us they got the same simple message. You had to take care of yourself. First. Foremost. Clean yourself. Feed yourself. School yourself. Contain yourself. This wasn't harshly done, it was a matter of expectation; her will for them to take the reins was stronger than their resistance.

"You're here now. I can't change where you came from, I don't make the decision where you might go next, I can only tell you that you are here now. You're here. Focus on that. Start in your room here. There's Bedding Shelves down the hall that have all kinds of sheets, blankets, quilts, sleeping bags. Take what you need up to your room and make your bed. That's your first step to being here, making your bed."

"Hey, Lady. Ain't that, like, your job?"

"No, my job is helping you see that making your bed is, like, your job."

It was Jared's inspiration to offer some sleeping bags in the Kids' bedding choices. There's something comforting about being zipped in, snuggled down, without the fussiness of covers and sheets. He himself spent about a year sacking out in a sleeping bag when he was eleven, it was his night skin. He felt manly and rugged crawling into the sleeping bag (good to -35°, in case of a sudden Ice Age in his room). Sleeping bags were a great excuse to buy a super-washer for the Place. The ease of "making your bed" by flattening out your sleeping bag every morning was exchanged for the responsibility of washing and drying your sleeping bag every ten days.

Caroline designed a special section of the laundry room, she included wire drying shelves and a hanger rod in a cabinet that used the heat from the dryer drum to provide no-tumble drying, the dryer vented into the drying cabinet and was vented out of there through an exterior window fan drawing moisture with it. The Cabinet was seven feet tall, and it used the idea of a bread warmer to exploit the run-off heat of an electric dryer. All the Kids thought it was cool, which pleased her in a pre-verbal sort of way; she watched the older kids build it in the shop under my supervision. She thought she was dull and dreary to the Kids because she thought they couldn't see inside her to where her interesting bits resided. Thinking of improving the dryer was dull but to devise a solution and implement it was cool, these rare confluences strengthened her identification with the Kids. Otherwise, she was our whispering wind, here then not here; you notice a breeze as it passes.

Jared and Caroline knew not to talk about the Kids to other people, except in the most general terms of being affiliated with a social service site. The Kids were not to be considered a source of entertainment. Rose was adamant that the Kids Place not intersect with our town life. It wasn't only her children who needed to detangle from the Kids craziness, she knew she had to break away and let that world roll on without her direct attention. Good and bad were intense for the Kids; the Hardeens had earned a quiet steady existence at their own house no matter what job their mother happened to have. Jared and Caroline triangulated their City existence through their Mom, through me, and through Mrs. Dubicek.

Book II – Family. Life.

Mrs. D had a European sense of childhood as one of evolving obligation to hearth and home, to country, and to God Above. She had a busy life scouting merchandise for her seashore store, she had a snaking route to stores she knew all over the country. Caroline was her work-from-home assistant, researching the value of pieces that became available, helping re-pack and ship catalog sales from their office in the barn. Jared appreciated Mrs. D's sense of formality towards his budding man-ness, she conceded his privacy in return for higher expectations of his social behavior.

In this way, my life with Rose was rich, mellow. Amidst all this energy from other people, we were able to complete our own circuit, interlock and cycle. Nothing in my life had prepared me for the entirety of marital love. I'd been intermittently intimate, haphazardly trusted, time proved these relationships had not been sufficient to satisfy my desire to bond with another human being. I never really had a father, or a brother, or sister, aunts, uncles, cousins, MOTHER. It was no wonder the fullness of having a wife dazed me.

Rose had conflicting memories of her early married life, with the ill-suited pretty boy who spawned not fathered her kids, but the newly-weds had been too young and silly to understand what it meant to establish a household. They rented cheap apartments with faulty appliances and wacky neighbors, the honeymoon lasted until her morning sickness started. She began to grow up but her ex-husband did not, they bickered their way to the five-year mark when she got pregnant with Caroline. She fought to get free of him (resisting her own fear of being on her own was harder than opposing his threats if she left him). Her long fight for independence, with two kids, gave her plenty of time to consider what she needed in a life mate. Kind, even-tempered, accomplished. She did tuck away some of her most tender honeymoon love memories, nursing an eloquent hunger for the glory of physical love. Rose understood procreation on the socio-biological level like most of us do but she also held a strong sexual ego and presence. She never repudiated that part of her, even if circumstances did not allow her to celebrate it. Our courtship rituals were mature as befit a mother of two adolescents and a near-forty bachelor; however, we found ourselves leaning into our kisses, drawing tighter into our hugs, carefully aligning our proverbial "teeth" in the "zipper" of our love. We were looking to bag a life mate. Neither of us needed to fill in financial gaps with our relationship, we each had stable housing, and suitable sites for meeting; the only reason to come together was personal pleasure. If we took our time with the alignment, our zipper would run up/down and we'd be skin to skin alone.

Mrs. D allowed us to forget the kids for up to a day at a time, it was this freedom that sealed the romance between us. No parent relaxes when the kids are out of sight unless they are assured they know where the kids are and what is happening there. Whether on a school field trip, or at a sleep-over at a friend's house, custodial parents have to *know* where their kids are. Mrs. D was *in loco parentis* just as my grandmother had been for me while my hippy-chick mother wandered the highway looking for Deep Meaning. We only had to know where Mrs. D was to know our kids were still on radar. We did the same in reverse for her, when she went on scouting trips she knew there were people who tracked her progress, who could say what town she was expected to be in within any few hours. She was cautious in her travel arrangements but lax in her personal contacts. She liked to chat and we worried she might reveal her vulnerabilities to a con artist or worse. We didn't want to challenge her, exactly, we wanted to be assured by her that she shared our compartmentalization ethic. Family was not discussed at work, our life here wasn't described to people on the road except in the broadest terms (she lives with some people, some of whom are kids, shared with a cat, birds, a dog part-time).

This structure left Rose and me free to disappear together, which is the essence of courtship, to travel tandem, whether it was to the symphony or a clam bake at the shore or an estate sale… we did whatever we did together, apart from any others who were or weren't doing the same thing we did. We looked through each other's eyes and saw more, felt more, knew more than we ever had when we had been apart. Love. We fell in love. Poetry and music and art museums and shipping docks were changing backdrops to the Love Orbit. Caroline named this Parallel Universe one night when Rose and I were serving up Boston Baked Beans, I held the heavy pot and she dipped the ladle, our eyes met and held and we forgot what we were doing, her lips softened, mine set. Tick tock went the clock. Caroline piped up, "Give up on getting beans, brother. They've fallen into Love Orbit." Jared gagged, Sovereign barked from his rug, Rose and I returned to the mundane world of hungry kids and hot food… Caroline had pegged us. Our love was zipping up and down, open and closed, enfolding and releasing us, showing how easy it was for us to access that intimate cordiality we trusted to be love.

Rose was kicking butt at the Kids Place, using the lasso of her experience to restructure the workings of a faltering care center. Staff had to be sorted between keep and go, facilities were assessed, financials analyzed. She was going to leverage the combined budgets of her dependents' subsidies into a *place* for Kids. She didn't even get involved directly with the Kids until she'd settled into the role as Executive Director (although it was hard for her to wait, I know). Her first goal had been to make the place conform to its legal and fiduciary duties; it wouldn't serve anybody if it bankrupted itself, or broke standards. She then met with the current population. She wanted to make the statement that the Kids Place existed beyond and outside of any particular Kids, that it was a *location* that consolidated *services* for the good of non-voting citizens meaning them, the *people* in this room today, and tomorrow – yes, they were young but each day brought them closer to adulthood where this protection ended. The residents weren't misled that this was home, and Rose was not playing mommy. Rose steered the Kids Place as if it were a sea-going vessel, things were ship-shape, quarters were squared away. Count on it. She was more shaman than tyrant, things just went her way. Her advice was solicited because to do otherwise ran the risk of failure through circumstances she saw that you might have missed. She had the power to nip choices in the bud. Because dithering wasted money, she kept your eye on the outcome, you had to balance both immediate and long-term results. Methodical application of the rules governing custodial care of minor children gave Rose resources to provide housing, guidance, options, to Kids who fell off a family wagon.

Rose thought the essence of a family could be contained in a prairie wagon, larger than a car, frailer than a train, containing the members and their most precious possessions, their cookery, their books, their bedding. Sometimes a child was flung clear of their own family wagon, bounced onto the vast expanse of prairie/mountain/canyon. If they were lucky, they got picked up by the community wagon train. She didn't let herself dwell on the pathologies of the families that spewed these Kids into the system, because that wouldn't advance her cause. She took one place and made it safe.

Rose's talent was providing a conduit for other people's talent to emerge, it let her be a fantastic parent and a commendable employee; she got great results with a straightforward approach. She had an honest appreciation for ability of almost any kind. Once she knew your ability, she could spot your utility. It is the same in our marriage; she has a graceful way of opening my potential and allowing me to shine. I am her love, her precious, her honor… I touch her heart from the inside.

Passion started as such a sad word, the abjectness of Christ's sorrow and pain and hope bleeding through his wounded soul. *Passion* weakened until we now say we have a passion for ice cream… a word diminished in the vernacular, too often associated with sex not love. My passion for my wife Rose is tender and terrified, so much could be wasted, lost, if it is not nurtured. Our sense of a marital chamber is replicated in our three homes: town, shore and the A-frame on the Kids Place acreage. In each of these places there is one room with a locking door, with heavy drapes over sheer curtains, bare wood with scattered thick rugs, bed sheets with high thread counts because our love is worth the expense… in each of these chambers is a queen sized bed, a table for two, a flat strong one-armed sofa. God knows we love each other! We tuck ourselves away so that we can increase the intensity of our expression; we shut the world out because it would be dangerous to reveal our vulnerabilities to anyone but each other. It is the highest level of trust to strip, whimper, howl, to bare your flesh and show your feelings. It was selfish, we admit, to create these fortified zones of privacy but we felt we deserved them. We had waited a long time to fall in love with each other and patience created the reward of release.

Rose stayed slender through the years, and I avoided gaining weight as it would have strained my hip replacement, so even in our middle age we offered the best opportunities for physical connection. Her breasts were small but heavy just like I thought, the basin of her hips was wide and firmly set; my legs were strong and I had broad shoulders so that I felt as if I could shelter Rose in my embrace. We were beautiful with each other, sharing a sense of stamina in our lovemaking. Our schedules were hectic, we were always on the move, but we stole away to be together. Morning delight, nooners, skip-dinner-sex, it all stemmed from our pledge to share the best of ourselves.

I never had any hang-ups about sex unless you count the fact I thought it was too precious to waste on strangers; I was lucky to have had great girlfriends and we explored aspects of love. With Rose, those facets melded into something denser than its pieces. We could slap and tickle, wrestle and writhe. Even in our shyness there was the twinkle of temptation. Perhaps it helped that we had both been fasting, in the sexual sense, before we approached our physical relationship. It was all new to us again even as we were reacting to other things we'd done, things we'd read, things we'd thought. Manifesting before our eyes, our love formed itself as a deep joy, and we were happy to be alone together. I brushed her hair, she rubbed my back, I bathed her after she sullied herself with me. I was the big bad wolf, deep beneath my Mr. Nice Guy persona, chained by loyalty to a soft lady with a sharp heart.

We weren't likely to be cheaters, we were too aware that cheating is for cowards. It takes strength of character to face down the lure of change and the pull of curiosity. Rose and I were too tender-hearted to punish each other with senseless mistakes, you do not cheat by accident. Our marriage vow prized commitment even in the face of disappointment – we had discussed this before the wedding. It was a second level of pledge, clarifying what our faithfulness meant to each other, beyond the generally accepted meaning of the words. Fortune may change, circumstance may change, but this simple vow not to forsake each other rang out.

I know in my heart we don't really live together, not like the couple that has one house, one car, one schedule to share. We have days apart from each other, and times we are apart from the children, which makes for a freer sort of acceptance. Sometimes I think it is harder for true lovers to be together all the time than to be apart, ardor is too hot (tangy) to absorb without relief. Our business interests were not the only excuse for our absences, some part of each of us wanted to be alone to savor what we wrought together.

At the Kids Place, since each of them had their own room, it was decided that the room could be a barometer of their equilibrium. We weren't sneaky about it with them, they were told that they were minors in our custody and as such we could search anywhere at any time, it was good faith that we wouldn't if we didn't believe we had to; except for the room-numbers-drawn-from-the-hat weekly inspection. If the Kid couldn't muster enough energy to present an organized room, then we had legitimate reason to worry about them. Especially if we had described what we would accept so they could "fake" it (if the effort of faking it is sincere). My grandmother had pioneered the concept when she explained to my long-ago teen self that if my room didn't alarm her when she stepped in to put my clean laundry on my bed then she'd leave me alone about it. I could have a messy closet if its door could close, I could lump clothes on my bed if the spread was pulled up and tucked under the pillows. She was smart enough to grant me privacy while maintaining my sense of being monitored, so that I grew to trust myself.

Putting this philosophy into action had worked with Jared after one hellacious night when Rose invaded his room and cleaned it. Dirty dishes, sodden socks, candy wrappers, muddy shirts, an empty milk carton, all of it mixed together on the floor, under his bed, in his dresser drawers.

She'd been after him to take care of it and finally she said that he was mistaken to think it was his prerogative to live in filth – he'd have to wait until he could afford his own place to trash. She could negotiate clutter but she wouldn't tolerate a health hazard. She started in the northwest corner and worked to the south edge. She had a trash bin, a laundry basket, a charity box – and his things were flying into them. Jared was shocked, he'd been jollying her along about cleaning his room, figuring her complaints were just mother-noise, but watching her churn through his belongings scared him, she was mad (she was right) and she was taking action.

"Here's the deal, Jared. I'm cleaning this room and deciding what stays and what goes. You gambled and lost your vote. Once it's clean, we start over. You make the bed, put dirty clothes in your hamper, keep the floor clear then I'll leave you alone about your room. If you won't do that, then I'm going to clean it again, and next time I'll be tougher about what I toss since you can't seem to manage caring for this many nice things. Eventually, if you don't get the idea, you won't have anything left to clean…"

"Whatever. Mom. I get the message."

"Get this – if you don't want me treating you like a ten-year old then quit acting like one. If you want me to give you 'mommy' service like putting your laundry away and picking up your trash then you aren't getting teen-age privileges. When I see you treating your room like a pig sty then I'll know you're telling me you're out of control, you aren't capable of maintaining yourself."

"So you're admitting to me that what's important to you is outward appearance?"

"Oh, yeah. In life, outward appearance is your first level of communication. You neutralize the first reaction and you have the chance for a deeper, more satisfying expression of yourself."

"Isn't that superficial?"

"That's the point. People see the surface first. If you want freedom, look like you're following the rules. You pass the superficial barriers that way. Cops don't stop you, teachers relax… a smart individual uses the herd to protect him, understanding its strengths to exploit them."

"That sounds kind of hopeless."

"Look around you, buddy. There's misery, yes, and most of it avoidable. You're getting a good start in life…"

"… I know that, Mom."

"… which you could squander. Lots of jerks got started in good homes, and plenty of heroes rise up from the street. You're not a little kid anymore. Like it or not, you really are a teenager. Closer and closer to becoming a man. Your choices are starting to count. You could father a child…"

"Mom!"

"… kill somebody with the car, flunk classes you need to pass to advance to go where you think you're going, you are choosing experiences to have. You keep saying you want to be treated with respect, fine, do something respectable."

"So, like, if my room looks OK on the surface then you won't feel the need to go into my dresser?"

"Yes. It's the real deal. If the room doesn't scare me at first glance then I won't wonder what else is going on in there. Show me you 'get' the camouflage of conformity. Respect the facts of life, you aren't saying you like them but you are saying you notice them."

"I'm old enough to be given some freedom."

"You're old enough to earn some."

The problem with adults and teenagers is that they exist at cross-purposes. Teens are hardwired to be foolish, obtuse, self-absorbed… they're in a second toddlerhood. Parents have spent a dozen years picking up the loose ends for this kid and now they have to learn to let the kid shoulder their own risks. It's tense because the teen has some legitimate gripes about the half-way status, too young to be childish and not old enough to be adult. The adult remains legally responsible for junior which puts an edge on the situation. I'd known Jared long enough to differentiate his age-appropriate glowering from the sensible forward-moving boy he had been. I had every faith he'd pull it all together but it was painful to watch. Rose had more problems with him, of course, because not only was she his "real" mother but kids often find it safer to challenge their Moms rather than Dads (step-dads) (mothers' husbands/boyfriends) ((uncles, granddads...)). He believed she stayed awake at night thinking of ways to humiliate him – as if she had the energy for that! I was glad I could step out of it at times, because I didn't like anybody disrespecting my wife, I took exception to his tone of voice, and I boiled over if he kept it up too long. This was their battle, my struggles with him were more distant and formal; he had a real Dad to compare himself to, he was quick to remind me, tossing this familiar bomb whenever he wanted to dodge me.

Jared had to reduce Rose's power over him, he couldn't hope to be all-knowing and super-competent when he faced adulthood... so he had to find her flaws to reassure himself that *even if flawed* it was possible for a person (her, hence him) to survive, thrive. It's a silly phase because the bitter fact is your parents were here first and have more rights than you do. (The balance will shift later.) Don't waste your time tilting at that windmill, get concrete with your situation, face it and tame it, know it. The goal isn't to get free, it's to stay free.

We had to induce this philosophy artificially at the Kids Place, not only because they weren't with their biological/custodial parents but because, when they had been, their situations had not been successful. They saw their grown-ups failing, falling... why should teens listen to somebody who couldn't get their own act together? They saw tired cops and harsh teachers and creepy neighbors, they found little to respect. The Kids Place had to run on respect, it was the best medicine to give and get. We established basic rules and enforced them uniformly. It sounds like a simple plan but we struggled with it every day as the kids and staff found new ways to test each other. Conflict wasn't all the Kids' faults by any means, we had counselors that were ill-suited to their jobs, we had a hard time maintaining a healthy mix of adults to supervise the Kids. We had the nightmare of predators, the tragedy of the good people who died young. Our own involvement had to be explained again and again as each new Kid tried to figure out prevailing conditions. The hardest part was not picking out special cases, in order to succeed overall we had to take and hold the role of general custodians. We saw that every Kid got the exact share of attention deserved by each of them. Kids with disabilities took more physical care, of course, but that was handled by the therapists and aides, we let the psychologists work on their psyches... and for legal reasons we didn't hug or kiss them. That was tough with the little ones, we made sure to establish ways to communicate our pleasure with their behavior, we colored and we puzzled and we played endless board games, spending the time to prove our acceptance of them.

I sympathize with school teachers and health workers who fear their well-intentioned affections can be misinterpreted, it is natural for humans to express attachment with physical contact. Too bad the wicked have ruined it for the kind, at the expense of the kids who deserve better. The adults have failed to find reliable signals to keep the big bad wolves away from the piglets, at least until the piglets get big enough to run away in the hopes that someday they'll grow big enough to turn and fight back.

Some of the Kids were already sexualized by the time they joined us, this made it especially critical to keep horny folks away. The combination of youthful purity and manipulative attraction can short-circuit a selfish adult's judgment; allowing them to convince themselves they aren't doing with they are doing: corrupting. We as a species apparently prize our youth, we try to shelter them, hope to usher them toward the future we want to give them. Life doesn't make it easy, it jumbles hormones & neurons into the flowering of the pre-adult, leaving behind the husk of a child, forever set by conditions beyond its own control. Adulthood is a launching but launching is only the start of the real journey; it's easy to look back and wish you'd had a better start (different start) but it is healthier to look forward and improve your momentum.

Formalizing my view of the transition from dependent to independent took (most of) the heat out of my reaction to Jared. He was literally wired differently than a child, new pathways burned in his body and in his mind; he was as yet not shaped into an adult. Certain bridges did not exist in his brain yet; love it or hate it, that rush of youth is only one stage of a bigger process. He played it cool with me, and that's where I left it.

Caroline was pretty much frustration-proof, whatever Jared did was observed, noted and forgotten. Good, bad, indifferent, it was just the many faces of her beloved brother, and if he got some sort of relief by mocking her girliness then she was glad to be a help. She was surprisingly steady when you judged her by her progress. She pointed herself in a direction and kept pushing on. Mrs. D was her Elder Woman, a trader of goods, something that Caroline found worthy at an existential level. This girl wasn't going to be anybody's servant, she was born a merchant. She and Mrs. D were free of the mother-daughter strain which liberty invited camaraderie. They were deeply patriotic, the serious citizens of the household, true believers in the "Neighborhood Watch". They lived in a small-focus world of things acquired, things sold, things traded.

Jared's life was a mini hot zone, a turf war every day. He woke up one morning outraged that the school had such a high ratio of chaperones to students at the dances and bowling parties. As if being gathered in a gym (or bowling alley or skating rink or national park) with a young herd in high scent, neighing and braying at each other, running fast in no particular direction, showing gait not aim, was the sort of evening every adult longs to experience.

"We aren't *allowed* to let you loose, Jared. It's a legal thing – we supervise you because we have to."

"We aren't doing anything wrong."

"You just do it too fast and too loud sometimes. Parents are out on the boundaries of these activities, we aren't as interested in what's happing between you, what concerns us is how you interact with the outer world. There's more going on than you're aware of sometimes. We're looking out for you."

"We don't need any help."

"You don't have credit cards to pay for the movie, you can't drive yourself to ski practice or sign the waiver when you get there – adults provide access to places you couldn't gather otherwise. Admit that, work with it. We have to co-exist because the law says so, you deserve food and shelter and opportunity and we determine how those things are defined until you're old enough to do so for yourself. We pick the house, cook the food, apportion the money and time."

"I'm trapped in your world."

"Temporarily, but we're showing you a way out, what started as a womb and turned into a crib then became a play pen enlarged by yards reaching out to the streets... we let you get farther and farther away. You still have to dock back at home every night, but your 'territory' is growing, you've got greater range. Trouble and Fortune lurk, mimicking each other. You don't know who to trust."

"We trust each other."

"Irrelevant, the danger adults worry about is not only between you kids, it's all around you, you need to pull together and protect the group, be smart and alert, because you're playing for keeps."

"Heavy, Jerry, dead lead heavy."

"So is regret. It thuds into your life and doesn't go away. You're edging into the land of no do-overs."

The call for a head-on wreck came in about three in the morning so I guessed it was drunk driving, and since they needed two tow trucks I figured it was going to be ugly. Jared was spending the weekend with me, because Caroline and Rose were accompanying Mrs. D to Reno for a Doll Collector's Rally. He had heard the phone ring and he appeared in the kitchen, dressed for the road. I didn't want him to go but he argued that he'd stay in the truck unless I signaled for his help, that he'd respect the privacy of the accident victims, and, besides, he really wanted to be available in case I needed him. This was another case of having to extend myself into Jared's life – I didn't want him to see a decapitated body (even a loose hand is upsetting), at the same time I thought seeing the scene around such things can temper the risk of being involved in a collision. If he wasn't old enough to come along with me, was he really safe when left

Book II – Family. Life.

alone at home? This wasn't a scene for Sovereign so we left him to guard the beach house.

I let Jared come with me, not stressing the conditions that he lay low, hang back, be cool, because it was too important for him to prove himself to me. He was accompanying me on an adult mission and his behavior had to be allowed to express itself. He was keyed up on the way, but he refrained from asking for details. I was in radio contact with a cop at the scene and she was pressing me for my ETA. No need for her to tell me to hurry, her concern about my arrival time said it all. Somebody was in need of immediate assistance. She said the car had flipped over and the roof had crumpled so the occupants were trapped inside. I could crank open a door and rip off a roof but I couldn't remove the undercarriage of an upside-down vehicle. The window frames were distorted, it was hard to trust them to prevent the passenger compartment's further collapse although they did have some jacks in place to at least slow the fall if they did fail. Jared stayed in the truck while I shined my light inside the upended car, noticing there was a lot of blood, I heard some rattling breaths that sounded sad. The fire truck was on its way, it had pneumatic power to inflate "steel-ribbed floats" that could lift the car so they could extract the victims. The other car was across the road crunched against a tree, the front seat shoved into the engine compartment while the back seat and trunk were intact. The cop shook her head at me, directing my focus to people we had some hope of helping. I felt sick, it's hard for a guy who loves vehicles to see them used for suicide/homicide. Physics always prevailed. A moving object hitting a stationary object dissipates that energy violently.

"Jerry, I've taken all my pictures, what can we do to prep for the fire truck?"

"I'll have Jared place more flares before the bend – can you pull the squad car farther north to give the truck room to manuever?"

"This wasn't a head-on. I looked at the skids, these people were banking up for the turn, they got slammed at the exact moment for them to flip over. If they'd been on the straight-away it would have been a spin out. I think the other car lost it on the turn and clipped this car's back end at just the right angle to point itself toward that tree. That's the only big tree on that side of the road."

"Who's in the other car?"

"Two. Guys, I think."

"No chance..."

"... none."

Jared kept his eyes averted from the death car, after glancing at it when I asked if it looked familiar. He shuddered, no, and walked off with the flares. I wasn't sorry I'd brought him, I think all citizens should rotate through accident duty, to share the burden. There were two dead people, at least, a result of driving decisions. In many accidents, the second vehicle did nothing to cause the problem. They are broadsided, hit by a wrong-way driver, spun into. It sometimes takes two to tango, drag racers have high speed crashes, and it's harder to feel sympathy. I'd given up on wondering how drunks justified driving, and concentrated on the sober portion of the population who let it continue. I'm all for felony penalties on this form of maiming and murder, yes... the first time. No freebies.

I strung tarps around the car embedded in the tree; the local paper would be on the scene soon, I rarely had more than ten or fifteen minutes to sort things out before they showed up. The fire truck was placing the "floats" while the paramedics reached in and took pulses, counted respirations, assessed the possible complications of changing the victims' positions. Jared stayed back at the truck, alert for a summons, eyeing the firefighters, the cop and the two troopers, me, but not the cars. I know he thought about his childhood friend, Eli, who had been killed by a drunk driver. (He said he thought of it every time he heard about a car crash but this night he understood the <u>scene</u>.) The "floats" were inflating and the car groaned as the undercarriage was urged upward. There was a sudden pop of released metal and one of the victims pumped blood out the window, some part of his circulation system that had been pinched closed was released. There was a flurry of medical action resulting in the rapid extraction of the passenger. His arm was tied off but the damage was done, he'd lost a lot of blood, and they trundled away urgently, seeking the medical facilities in their ambulance. The driver was still unconscious; there was the faint echo of a moan in her every breath, as if her deepest self knew it was in pain before her brain reorganized enough to sort out the chaotic signals. The atmosphere was incredible, lights were pulsing, the air smelled of hot engines, blood, topped by the lilac scent from a nearby bush in bloom.

Once they pulled out the driver and got her into the ambulance, everything slowed down. Mobilized, they flew into the night, wailing, taking the frantic pace with them. The fire truck was disengaging itself from the scene, the cop was filling out paperwork; I went over to ask Jared if he wanted to help me hook up the flipped vehicle. He wouldn't be coming back when I returned to haul off the death car. First, the medics had to recover what they could of the people who'd been pulverized in it. Then they had to wrap the car so I could haul it to the police lot. There, it would be analyzed and sanitized, ultimately loaded on a transport to the crusher. It was a challenge for Jared to deal with his actual proximity to the second car, a blot of tangible violence, a twisted version of a familiar object. It lurked just beyond sight and he knew it. He didn't say much.

This wasn't the time for a lecture, he was imprinting a new definition of life and death. Later the scene could be touched like a talisman, something he *knew*. People died in and around cars. Innocence was no protection. Accidents were the unintended results of deliberate actions, the unforeseen ricochet of choice on circumstance. He wouldn't have been seeing himself as a victim, since he believed he was invincible but, rather, he projected the injuries to people he worried about (Mom, Sister, Mrs. D, even me). That was more reliable motivation anyway (he was much more conservative about our well-being than he was about his own).

"My mom isn't going to freak out because I asked to come to the scene, is she?"

"No, not because you asked. She might not like me agreeing."

"Sorry."

"Her not liking it doesn't make it wrong, I let you come along because I believe you're ready to step up."

"I, uh, I didn't really look at that other car."

"I know. That's smart. You knew it was there, you could sense the darkness around it, the hopeless sense of a done deed."

"Uh huh, creepy sad. How do the medics handle that?"

"It beats me, it's like they care so much that they stop caring at the moment of need and do what has to be done, knowing it might be hurting you but they are serving your greater good… they filter out their personal reactions and make medical decisions. They become biological plumbers, bone carpenters, circulation mystics, figuring out the human machine that's broken down."

"Mom doesn't want me taking driver's ed until next semester."

"Well, you can't get your license until next summer at the earliest."

"But I could be practicing! So I'd be a better driver when I could drive."

"It's a good argument, Jared. Then think about this car we're hauling, they were driving the speed limit around a curve, knocked out of orbit unexpectedly, they didn't even have time to react."

"So how would practice have helped me there?"

"Not being on the road reduces your chance of being involved a car accident."

"At least they had their seatbelts on, right?"

"Yeah. They were as right as they could be, and that might have saved their lives. By the way, I donate the hauling fee for death cars to a church charity."

"You don't want to make a profit on something like that."

"Money is energy, you want to watch which way it's flowing."

"I get it, about the energy thing. I can tell when I'm going in a positive direction by how it feels. I just got a big bolt of caution toward cars. People say they know how dangerous cars are but I've really seen it."

"You're old enough to understand, then, that you can call us to pick you up, any where and any time, if you think you could be in danger in a car. We'll come and get you and give you a ride home, no questions asked, and that includes your friends too. Not just because somebody's drunk but maybe they're a show-off, or just in a bad mood. The car might have problems, could be too many passengers… whatever. Making a call like that is a smart move and we'd be glad of it. However, it's not a free pass. If you keep getting into those situations then we might ask you to explain how repeated rescue isn't proof of premature freedom. OK?"

"'K"

Mrs. Dubicek was fun to have around, she continued my Grandma's tradition of leaving the Hardeens alone in the evening then joining them for an end-of-day ritual. It was comforting for the kids to have this anchor while their mother and I forged new routines of our own. Middle-aged newlyweds living family style are hard-pressed to establish the right mix of giddy privacy and responsible participation. Even if we enjoyed more escape hatches than the usual blended family, the kids still had to change gears when I started sleeping over. I knew I wouldn't be slopping around in my underwear (that wasn't my style in any of my dwellings), but I did let them see my scruffy pre-shower self when I staggered out for a cup of coffee. The kids had always worn robes (or heavy sweat suits) when they were out of their bedrooms, in part because of their differing ages and genders, partly in deference to their elder roommates.

Having a resident elder did more than calm down the routine, it gave the two generations a tie-breaker, a co-conspirator, a sympathetic ear. It took some of the sting out of the inevitable conflicts as kids crawl, walk, stomp toward maturity. Even little Miss Caroline could give out a shout when she was finally crossed. It took a lot to get a rise out of her but it could be done. She was self-aware enough to know that she bugged others with her dreaminess so she cut them some slack for their own peculiarities. Still, if Jared hogged one too many prized treats, or Rose forgot her precious colored pencils *again* then she hurtled into the here-and-now to stick up for herself. It was comical, from a long range perspective, to witness our ruminative bovine turn into a spitting feline! Intense!! When real battles crossed to parent-child, the elder knew to hold back from either side, they were mere spectators even if, in the future, they might serve as referee. Parent-child conflict is a part of growing up for both.

Old ladies have a special place in my heart, of course, because there is an air of stamina and resilience. They may get brittle but they rarely wither like little old men can. If you birth the babies, tend the wounded, mourn the dead, then you're most likely going to have a deeper perspective on the importance of things. Men "do" things and women "are" things, men hammered the coffins and women carried the memories. She is grief and hope, he is fact and act. I'm not talking about the professional division of labor for money which puts men in charge of undertaking and hearse driving… I'm referring to the longer history of our dual-gender world. Twined ivy: one variety for growth and the other for endurance making a pair stronger than the halves.

Our conjugal passion proved so delightful that we didn't even mind the "silent nights" we spent when the kids were with us. Those times our sex was almost tantric, the slow pressure of yielding. Once I had turned the pilot light up on my sex life, I found it amazing that I had gone several years without serious sexual contact. It hadn't been difficult to do when I did it yet it seems impossible in retrospect. I don't see those years as wasted, I was sharpening myself, back and forth on the whetstone of life, rubbing off burrs, smoothing my edges. I want to believe that I would have risen to meet Rose's ardent love even if she'd been my first. It isn't true but it's nice to think so. My mistakes and false starts were no less important than my milestones. Women like Reed might not have been suitable as wives but they were worthy as partners. At the time. In the circumstances. I wasn't Mr. Right for them even if I was giving as much as I had at the time.

The acts of love are so inherently pleasing that they call out for re-creation, we want more of the same feeling even if it comes from different actions. Performing the part of honeymooners, Rose and I neck and

Book II – Family. Life.

pet whenever we get the chance, intoxicated by the right to have what has been wanted. We're hand-holding, hip-checking love birds. Caroline loves it, Jared tolerates it, Mrs. D. pretends not to be paying attention (although the sight of united citizens thrills her patriotic heart).

Caroline had been about nine when she finally got around to asking about the mysterious Mr. Dubicek. Mrs. D told her she'd have to wait until she was eleven to hear *that* story. Caroline accepted that as an answer until she was eleven, then she pressed for the promised explanation. Well, Mrs. D was born with the name Georgiann Dubiczewski, and lived a simple life in her native Poland. She was shipped to England in 1939 in a boatload of young scholarship students, supposedly to study abroad for one term but actually to evade the tightening noose of political genocide that would eventually destroy her family and render her a sixteen-year-old orphan. In the confusion of V-E Day, she finagled a boat ticket to America and finally stood at Ellis Island, relieved to have put the ocean between her and her dark memories. America was her new country and the gigantic bureaucracy in service to handing freedom to people like her seemed like fairyland. Exhausted civil servants truncated her name to George N. Dubicek during her immigration processing; she was not about to complain about what they called her as long as they stamped her paperwork and pointed her path deeper into the U.S. of A. She added the Mrs. later to make it clear she wasn't a man on her official documents. Caroline understood this as a plausible explanation but not really an answer – did it mean, then, that just because Mrs. D. had not been married then, that she had never been in love? Was she *Miss* George N. Dubicek? Ahhh... *that* story would wait until Caroline was fifteen.

I am a definite believer in pairing, and had very much enjoyed observing the richness of my grandmother's love for her second husband, it was just as obvious that a bad relationship is usually worse than no relationship. Too much murder-suicide in the "home sweet home" for me to believe everybody improves life by adding a partner. I had a pretty good idea what it took for the not-so-young "George Dubicek" to work her way across post-war America, I couldn't ask what sad details left her without a family before she was twenty? The part I know is her moving slowly from the European-immigrant East coast to the mixing bowl of the Midwest until she reached the Native-Hispanic-Islander-Black/White mix of the West, amalgamating a strong sense of fairness and security within herself. She had toiled in other people's retail shops, selling women's clothes and men's shoes and knockoff sportswear, until she had set aside enough of a stockpile to rent her own place at the shore, mixing tourists and townspeople into a steady circuit exchanging goods for money. I could see that she had been plainly pretty all her life, sometimes I thought of her as June Cleaver, trim and tidy, no outstanding feature to provide a physical focus. I knew she had enjoyed the attentions of a gentleman caller for a few years, I heard all about it at the poker games. (Men's gossip isn't catty, it's a dogged reporting of prevailing conditions.) Mrs. D told me later that the old coots had it all wrong, the man was homosexual, her true friend, they went places and did things because they liked each other, they held hands because they enjoyed human contact, and the long nights with the lights low were spent reading each other's Tarot cards – each hoping to get clues to their respective man hunts.

 It was an honor to serve as Mrs. D's family. No matter the details of how such a thing came to pass it remained true she was alone when I met her, tethered but not really connected. The store kept her busy, selling provided structure to her life. The ocean she faced now didn't touch her birthplace, the war had severed her from her homeland. Getting to know her so well itself was a lucky fluke, Rose and I had just started dating while we were at the shore one summer, and we were looking for a companion for Caroline on evenings that we went out. Jared was the one who suggested Mrs. D. (he knew too many babysitting girls his age who were not really paying attention to the kids in their care besides he didn't want them that close to his things). Even now, Jared watched not only the foreground but the background. We were living in a snow globe, we could shake things up but it was always the same flakes swirling around. We were content, certain we'd snapped together the pieces of an engaging puzzle.

Book II – Family. Life.

Then, in one day, Rose rippled into another dimension. She woke up wary and distant, distracted by some interior storm. I thought she might be sick, but if so then it was the opposite of feverish. She delayed her breakfast to take a walk, something she says she will do more than does, but that day she actually did. I watched her walk up the hill not knowing that another woman would come back and take her place. I made myself available to her and also left her room to maneuver. It wasn't scary, then, because my mind stayed at DefCon 5, maybe she might have caught the flu, problem would be solved when she snapped out of it. She remained, in my mind, the same dear Rose.

It was the end of summer, shoreline vacationers needed more help than ever to cram in last minute "excursions" <u>doing</u> *something*.... before it was time for school again! I was gone almost a week and sensed a shift in Rose when I got back to town. DefCon 4. On the surface, things seemed normal but I caught her looking at me, out of the corner of her eye, angled through the mirror, not reacting to my behavior, more like recording it. We moved up to DefCon 3 (uh-oh, she's evaluating me and I'm not sure which criteria she's using). I tested that theory and found it limited, she was doing the same thing to the kids, I flashed on the image of a farmer surveying crops, a rancher eying cattle. Mrs. D was using her summer rail pass for one last quick scouting, people closing up their summer homes dispose of the oddest things. Rose's alienating behavior was present for five or six days... a speck of time out of the years of being around each other, and now being together. I was sure this was something I had never seen. Ever.

Rose decided it was time to clean out the family closet, full of photos and school art projects and handy gadgets we forgot we had. This was no mere straightening, she made Jared remove the contents, and Caroline helped sponge down the walls. Rose then set to opening every box, sorting through all the things we'd put away, pictures of my Grandmother, of Wishbone, of us all when we were younger. This led to a rethinking of things on display and the next thing I knew the look of the house changed. I thought she might be reliving her past, comparing it to now, not sure if this outcome really signified forever. DefCon 2 (she's non-happy yet un-sad).

Mrs. D returned and loved the new arrangements, or so she said, but she shot me a look in the kitchen when Rose tied on her shoes for a walk. Day after day my wife trudged off, slow to start, dragging herself along, then, somewhere farther along, out of our sight, a new source of energy took over and she returned resolute, head high. She didn't have grandiose ideas, but I noticed the windows had been washed, there was a new cabinet in the laundry room, our bedroom became scented with the vanilla she bathed in, she was soaking and floating in the tub from what I could glean lurking outside the door – these weren't the teasing bubble baths of our early romance; she was grooming herself, and it wasn't for me. She loved me as much as she ever did... what an ambiguous way for me to see her seeing me.

Before I knew it, I was headed back to the shore for the post-Labor Day rituals of a vacation town. It was cleanup season, we were battening our hatches, setting ourselves against the coming winter, knowing the storms were beginning to form, they always did and always would. If we had the gall to stand at the edge of our land mass then we better learn to make structures that work with the winds and the water. Rose was supposed to join me that weekend and I wondered why I was wondering how it was going to be... I hadn't questioned it before but now it was like we were meeting all over again. DEFCON 1 (her thorns are showing). Our bodies maintained their harmonious accord, and we made our tender feelings known, my sweet wife, her hungry man. Otherwise, we were incommunicado. I wasn't invited into her thoughts, I was locked out with the kids and Mrs. D; Rose was preoccupied. At the shore, I understood that we were still learning about life together, and I shouldn't worry too much even though my instincts were screaming to veer off. Nobody was landing on Rose, our mother ship – we, her fleet, were waved away. I saw her gathering strength, or presence, but it was a solitary state, or, at least, exclusionary.

I can see this happen from that first walk in this non-stop series, I was right to go on high alert with her yet I was completely off-base in my

Book II – Family. Life.

reasoning. She'd been to this dark garden before, and she was about to pitch me into it.

Jared had retained his membership in Students Against Drunk Driving in honor of his friend Eli, and for his junior year community service requirement at school he decided he would help the road crew set up the SADD shows. They'd pull into a school parking lot and take over the gym/auditorium/cafeteria… introduce the students to people their age who had stories to tell, tear down the set and move on. Taking action calmed the crusader side of him and he was soon volunteering for political committee work passing out leaflets supporting harsher penalties for criminal driving. He made a victim portrait collage interspersed with mirror shards entitled "Them Yesterday, Us Tomorrow?". It was noble and forthright of him to attach his labor to his belief. He knew he was duly credited at home for his service hours so it was a good deal "financially" in his credit towards a car, but from our perspective it was going to make him a better driver and that was a wise move. Both elements moved him closer to car ownership.

I agreed with him about impaired driving (drunk, drugged, distracted, emotional, fatigued). Plain and simple, we're tolerating dangerous drivers at our own peril. We are maimed and murdered by these drivers, we literally live at their mercy; they feel free to aim themselves in a generally forward direction and pour on the gas. Worse, many of us are them at times. I made our tow service available on all the holidays, cooperating in the town's pool of ride-givers for notorious drinking events like St. Patrick's Day. Still, cleaning up reckless wrecks remained a year-round duty. I knew Jared was turning a corner and I was curious about his future. His ability to take his emotions and create change for others heralded a good heart, and it put him in touch with kids from various schools in the district, expanding his horizons beyond his own small pond in the neighborhood. His faint but definite mustache bristled in the sun, this beloved facial hair marking impending manhood. He and his peers were no more full of bravado than any other generation even if they were certainly freer to express themselves verbally, new millennium kids are polluted by beer commercials and car ads into thinking that buying those things got you those luscious models – and it was cool to say so. We raised the point it was just as cool to ignore all that and develop your own ideas.

Rose was giving him a long leash, he was still tethered to the family calendar and had to approximate his whereabouts, our shared family agenda was a necessary device for staying connected. He and his mother didn't seem to spend much time together but he wasn't complaining, he was enjoying his autonomy, still secure that he could be roped in if he went over his head. The house had been Battleground Teen Freedom for several years, until he got in it in his head that he could be as free as he could be. He was the one setting his own limits.

About that time I had to work a fatal roll-over on the four-lane north of the shore, I wondered if it was going to be possible to erase the images of a bloody new shirt, a gory purse. I was heartsick at the loss of life, realizing the disruption of some family line, more so having seen with my own eyes how precious Jared and Caroline were. They were truly related to me, through me. I was somebody they could count on. I was connected to them in a way I had shared with Grandma and with Carl, these people who lived their lives with me. Please let them never rip away from me. Travel, yes. Exile, no. Ascend... maybe later.

Rose asked me to meet her at a large chain hotel near the airport, she said she'd be sitting in the coffee shop. I would have expected her to lounge in the bar, a little naughty, seductive. That alluring Rose was not at this meeting. Instead, I was sipping tea, studying the orange rinds and nut husks on her fruit plate (a vegetarian's version of bones left after a meal).

"Jerry, I got us a room upstairs, I have the key. It would be nice if I could pretend we're here for some kiss and tickle. I mean, of course, we are. I do want to be alone with you. I have to warn you, perhaps I've gotten you here under false pretenses."

"I arrived at the appointed time, Rose, mind open. I'm suitably stocked for an overnight, or longer – or less. Am I being invited to join you?"

"Don't kid yourself, Jer, you're already strapped in and we're ready to roll."

She hooked her arm through mine and escorted me to our waiting suite, she had set aside a bag of groceries, some French bread, ginger ale, it all looked very motel-get-away normal. We could fall out in rented rooms, stripped of our liabilities, the thrill of sin sanctified. This time she sat at the table and held out her hand, palm up. I didn't want to hear what she had to say because she didn't want to say it. Her whole body resisted connecting with me so the outstretched hand was significant. I put my hand alongside hers, leaving her free to make another move, to better define her interest. Whatever had gone on before was over, and we were on the mark, get set and ready to go.

"Jerry."

"Rose."

"I really do love you."

"You show me you do."

"I don't want to hurt you… ever."

"Please don't."

"I'm in trouble."

"How can I help?"

"Well, that's what we're here to find out."

At that moment in our lives, I hit a new level of appreciation for the woman I married. I had been petrified that there was a situation that locked me out, when in fact it would turn out that I had locked in.

"We made a baby…"

"Baby?"

"Early June good for you?"

"You're pregnant?"

"Not officially. There's a test kit over in that bag, I thought we'd review the results together in the morning… you know, just the possibility of maybe having a baby is a big thought… let's not know tonight, not for sure."

"You've had longer to think this over. I'm spinning."

"Well, that's the hurtin' part, Jerry. It wasn't yours to decide, not equilaterally, not just because you say so. I decide if I'm going to try to physically grow a child in my body. Then I'll take your position into consideration. I promise, love, if you ever turn up pregnant, you can make your choice first."

"Jeez, Rose. I'm saying, wow. You know. I'm in a new world here."

"Let me give you the tour... I've been twice before."

Mrs. D and Caroline opened the Shore Shop Redux (Used Postpositively)... it was a combination curio depot and newsletter, the catalog was available in print and by e-mail. They shared hints on restoration, trends in collecting, guest columns, interspersed with descriptions of the types of items that might be available at the moment (the vocabulary lessons were free). They didn't promise to have everything you wanted, they didn't want to supply somebody's thirtieth Dresden doll, they provided the one brass ashtray that fit a reading corner perfectly. Sticks of incense would be tossed haphazardly in the bowl to discourage actual use, it was a prop, a sculpture, not a butt bin.

The cycles of life manifested themselves in the house – Caroline was in the first flush of her menses, Mrs. Dubicek was beyond that cycle and Rose was full-bore working her womb. Rose tells me that I have a sincere appreciation for women as "other"; I'm not a girly-man, she thinks I have a healthy respect for the mystery of life, why and how we as a people manage to keep our feet on the surface of the planet. I'm analytical, I like to have the facts so I can sense the trends in my life, how things work together, what I can count on. Women are a natural force like weather and geography, elements of the world. Men, too, carved their place on the face of the Earth. I was very interested in the pregnancy of my wife, in the life of my child, not sure of the outcome but enthralled (deeper than enchanted) by the process. Rose and I were surprised by this child, we had agreed not to do this, and had taken reasonable precautions. We were going to have to rework our life plan to extend child care from ending after Caroline's teens to lasting another twenty years... we could well be grandparents in that same time frame.

Book II – Family. Life.

We weren't telling people, in part because it is customary to wait out the first trimester, and in part because Rose needed time to shift her thinking. She'd already made up her mind to let the pregnancy roll forward, but she had to prepare for many possibilities of loss, consider miscarriage and stillbirth and sudden infant death syndrome through the many years of fear that you'd lose something more precious than your own life. I was only just getting a glimmer of this but she could remember and she could project.

"They hold us hostage, Jerry, we're offering ourselves up to protect the world from our newly formed spawn. We housebreak them, teach them manners, enroll them in school, discipline and shape them through the childish phases – it's never not your problem when your kid has a problem. I loved having little kids and I love having older kids, I just didn't think I was going to open that tiny door again. If I wasn't confident we really had tried to avoid this pregnancy, I'd be second-guessing my intentions. Here we are, chosen by some soul to deliver it to its destiny. Making a baby for our own growth would have been self-indulgent. To be selected by bio-lottery is beyond self-interested demand. It happens when it happens."

"We've got the money, we've got the time – that puts us in a comfortable position to take on the care and feeding of another family member. Rose, this baby picked us out; it isn't the other way around, we didn't order up a kid to serve a particular purpose in our lives together. I'm stunned. Jazzed."

"Can we talk about testing?"

"Amnio? Like that? Is it time for that?"

"It's too late for the early chorionic sampling, but I already decided that placental testing is too risky when I wouldn't do anything to stop the pregnancy, no matter the results. The fact of this life is not mine to decide."

"What if something could be done to improve the outcome? Wouldn't you give a child that chance?"

"This embryo is well-nourished, sheltered, and beloved. I've supplied all necessary vitamins and minerals, I'm faithful to fitness... I don't want to use bio-spy technology to interfere with the most private development of a life."

"There's still risk doing an amnio later, right?"

"Half a percent, one in two hundred… the problem I have with it is that it is an intrusion in fetal development. Pregnancy is growth sealed in the womb, it is nature's way to encase offspring in physical boundaries, beyond which nature will not let them go because they cannot survive… at what point do you stop them from being what they are set to be? Fix spina bifida with fetal surgery? Check for cleft palate? Assess potential height correlated from birth weight/length and distribution in adult population? Flavor their genetic soup to suit myself?"

"The flaw in that is you're choosing not to test for the same reason – to satisfy your concept of parenting. The fact is that the test can give you useful information, it can help you prepare."

"Think about what you're saying, Jerry, there are terminations associated with genetic testing, you peek into a process before it is finished. If nature wanted us to get a sneak preview we'd have a way to do that… there's a reason there is no such thing in mammals."

"So you oppose all surgery because it isn't 'natural'?"

"I object to deciding if some other being has surgery…"

"You're the boss of the baby, Rose. I want to understand where we're going even if I'm not in the driver's seat."

"Not quite so, co-captain. You have to step up for me and for the baby if something happens, what if I'm in a coma? What about the baby then? If I have cancer, do I delay treatment… what about an abruption?"

"I don't know. We don't even *know* that we're having a baby, isn't that what the pregnancy test is for? In the morning? What if it's positive, that's a good thing, right? We basically agree on that, don't we? That we would welcome a baby."

"Now I can say that and mean it. We can welcome a baby, not saying for sure there is a baby."

Book II – Family. Life.

Things change when you learn you're going to be a dad. I stopped calling Rose 'baby'. The endearment had been used with a sexual significance only, spoken in our intimate moments. She was the opposite of an adult male, the extent of which it took her pregnancy to reveal to me: she was not my infantile inverse, she was my feminine converse; she was my exact shadow even as she shifted shape. I rooted out some dark vein of presumption in myself about women, that sneaky escape hatch of men using gender but calling it sex as a marker of destiny (no one vital organ outweighs the other but if one did it wouldn't be the plumbing). The brain to think, the heart to power, the spine to carry... these make more difference in the outcome of our lives even if our outward emphasis on gender blurs that. If I'd rather be a smart woman (better) than a stupid man (worse), does that mean I'd really rather be a smart man (best) and would hate to be a stupid woman (worst)? Maybe this all went to prove I had too much time to think. Being in the tow truck, and the travel between our house and the Kids' Place, gave me lots of driving hours. I was able to relax the deeper part of my brain even as I sharpened my observations and reactions. It was important to me to calculate the trajectories of all the vehicles in my vicinity, always watching for points of convergence, avoiding them. If Rose asked, I might not remember half the trip, an hour or two lost, the driving automatic, the road known... meditative time.

I had been entered into one of life's strange states with impending fatherhood: having an existing fact (gender of baby) that would change my life not being known to me. The overall result of being a dad would be shaded by the gender of the child and, even though it was already determined, I wouldn't know until the birth. This really brought home the idea that the baby was already on its own path, we could lend energy but not provide purpose. Not knowing daughter or son, I had to open my heart double-wide which is a wonderful thing to do. Little girl/boy faces pinwheeled in front of me, I didn't know which one I'd see when the child heralded itself, when this one baby came out from the body cavity it had hijacked from me then would abandon for me to recover, facing their existential hostess in the breakthrough moment from unborn to born which starts our aging. You are measured from the moment of your emergence, and your mother will forever bear the marks of delivery so deep inside that they survive even death.

Rose was noncommittal about her expectations, husbanding her own energies in a sobering demonstration of self-sufficiency. She was carrying a child, to and fro, in her every moment; it took over more and more of her attention, captivated her physically, triggered resource retention (fat and water), the fetus was foremost a consumer of energy provided by her. She would never not be this baby's mother, while I remained at this stage a one-dimensional father. She enveloped the baby. I had finished my biological contribution in mere minutes many weeks ago, the rest of my choices were acculturated, fathers in my tribe were expected to care for the family and I stood proud and ready to do so. People teased us old folks about our young love, and we had to concede that we weren't poster-worthy parental models. We looked too sensible, too settled. The embryonic soul seeks asylum in the body of a woman who lives in one certain home, trusting that certain home will provide protection thus opportunity. Life wants to live, we want to live life, and it all starts with the portal of your mother's history when you are born. It is one specific year, you are in one specific place, there are circumstances. Geneva 1942. Cambodia 1968. This tethers you to a "here and now" point of consolidation. Infinite time can be divided (before you were born, after you died) with the interval between the two insignificant when we see the incalculable vastness of how long we aren't a living force. In the end we're each a little bump in the road quickly pounded back into the non-being of history and future... but oh how thrilling an interlude it is.

My little kid, my boy/girl child, was already on its way, much of its future determined by the twining of chromosomes, the helix of Rose Hardeen and Jeromeo Clover becoming a being never seen before, or to be seen again. I was superstitious enough not to voice my fears, I wouldn't even utter words in my head about them. I was resolutely open-minded as to the outcome of our handiwork. I had many positive images

Book II – Family. Life.

of children so it was easy to see how I could fit myself around the needs of one. I'd been lucky in my life and was willingly sharing that. I give to the child the chance for a future, at any cost to me. I say my life is big enough to provide shelter and care, a duty not lightly taken when you realize just how much goes into supplying a kid with everything for years and years. *Every thing.* Every meal, every blanket, every shoe, every sheet. If we don't provide these things directly, we put the child in situations that provide access. We equip our schools, communally fund our parks, we take care of our children overall. The cases of abuse and neglect rightfully offend us, because we don't accept an adult depriving a child of a future. We would rather see a parent surrender the child than destroy it. The child is of value in and of itself, no matter the current situation of the parent(s). Crack addict? Bank robber? Alcoholic… workaholic? Religious or hedonist? Details fade before the fact that if the parent fails in the duty of care then they are asked to declare it to be so and give up the child.

My kid was provided for into the foreseeable future. I'd stacked the deck in our favor, guaranteed to the extent possible a home and food and clothes, whether I was there or not, barring only the most grievous social upheaval that would wipe out the fail-safe systems of insurance, trusts, convertible cash, and holding companies I'd assembled. Our baby was graced/saddled with the kind of dad that took parenting seriously. I was going to take part in the shaping of _____ Hardeen Clover.

 Naming a baby! Naming a baby you have never seen, discussing the merits of multi-syllables, alliteration, history, popularity. Rose and I agreed to wait until we saw the baby, deepening the mystery of its gender, finding genderless nicknames to avoid using pronouns. The baby was never "it" between us, we always used a noun: bug, dot, bulge, soul, bio-pod passenger, tax deduction – all the ways you peg a real kid who doesn't yet have an identity.

We knew we couldn't see around the corners, that was the thrill and the horror of pregnancy. Rose grew her belly, she cradled herself, continuing her daily walks that had heralded her body's ascendancy.

We had been heart-and-soul newlyweds, and now we were husband and wife awaiting child. I envied her experience; she knew I'd have my first child only once, this once, something she had done and could not do again, something she could not do with me.

She also had tasted the joy of a successful birth, twice. Statistically, it is noted that if parents sire one of each gender they often stop at two children, while two children of the same gender were more often joined by a sibling... as if we desire to parent one *at least* of each... she had raised a boy, she had raised a girl... this new child was carving space into a heart the mother thought she had already filled. The years of building her strength had prepared Rose to carry the influence that pregnancy has on the mother's life. It is a physical-spiritual activity fraught with significance. It is hard not to notice who is truly pregnant and who is not obviously pregnant. The organic nature of pregnancy amazes. She is not pregnant alone, she has the product of the process seeking substance through her. In her third pregnancy, Rose knew that this was going to be weird for her, to not fear for the baby's basic safety like she did with her first two kids, back then she was scared she'd trapped innocent children in her low-down stage of stupid choices. She had feared she was selfish knowing they weren't getting two real parents, she knew her then-husband would never go the distance – something she didn't originally suspect because he started their marriage with such a flourish. No wonder... he had no intention of sustaining it. You chased the chick (high energy), you married the woman (low energy).

This pregnancy was welcome, there were no limits to resources, there was space and time available. A welcome pregnancy is an infatuation that is a mere precursor to the way you fall in love with your kid. The allure of new beauty on a familiar face, change on the surface and in the laugh, evolution in progress, genetic legacies being built. Rose had "caught" the baby, now she had to "carry" it before she eventually "dropped" it, literally unleashing it from its placental dependency, setting them both free but only momentarily, they reconnect eye-to-eye and skin-to-skin (nipple to lip), imprinting the essence of that which they will love. There is an outré-verbal declaration of possession, the special language that cackles in the looks between infant and parent.

I saw all this on the gentle curving sweep forward of my pre-birth fatherhood, when the brewing child was only a topic, shielded from me by own wife, she was hiding my kid in her belly, in secret communion translating my spermatozoidal hopes into a corporeal being. I had given Rose my name and now she gave me a child to march that shared name into the future. We weren't going to dead-end on the Hardeen-Clover family tree.

Jared took extreme exception to curfew when he was sixteen, he didn't have any wild and crazy activities to hide, he just wanted to hang out with his friends, taking turns being at each other's houses, including ours. Why did he have to be home, or them gone, by 10 on week-days and 11:30 on weekends? It was just plain stupid, and anybody who thought that curfew was important was, by logical extension, not to be insulting, he had to say it, they were just plain stupid too. He wasn't a wind-up robot who keeled over so early, like some eighth-grader! He was a high school guy, he knew when to go night-night.

We had to fall back on the "good of the many" versus the "good of the one", because his comings and goings had an impact on the rest of us. Both Caroline and Mrs. D were settled in bed by about 10 o'clock, and Rose liked a quiet house in the hours before midnight. These were the craziest battles, sometimes he was just being contrary, and if we told him he couldn't come home before midnight, he'd have urgent need to be in his room at 10:45. The reverse-inverse psychology wars ratcheted up and down around key issues like responsibility versus freedom and intention versus accomplishment. The constant skirmishing wore us down but the baby was a great reminder that stages of life are temporary so we didn't sweat his outbreaks of teen fever as much as we would have if we had time to ride him any tighter. He was a good kid with some gaps and lapses in judgment but he was learning his limits and abilities in the safety of our stable home. He thought the baby was a wonderful diversionary element and was solicitous in an absent-minded way. Our teenage girl-person was skipping up the straight and narrow, nailing the grades, loving the on-line store, maturing into a loyal fighter. Caroline was a kid activist for the parks department, faithfully attending park rallies around the City, adding to the clamor for safe yet challenging play spaces and green zones. Like Jared's volunteer work against drunk driving, her school community service started her on this path and I was glad they each looked out onto the world the way they did. This would pay off all their lives.

I confess that as the pregnancy progressed I expected to feel some urge to panic, on the order of thinking to ask myself 'isn't it time to panic?' so I'd race my thoughts but nothing caught me up, I was through-and-through accepting of something I thought I'd never be given or share… an heir. All my logical arguments against fathering a baby were valid, and I had felt good about that choice. I was equally pleased with the chance to have another choice. I was just like every decent father back to the cave-guy who did a better job of sheltering his young than the other cave-guys. Your father plays a pivotal role even if it is as an absent father, over-involved is as dangerous as under-involved, you may be a certain kind of dad but that is complicated by the fact you have a certain kind of kid to deal with. Life begins three-sided as mother-self-other which is one reason males have a feminine side and females need testosterone (in small doses). Your mother is the litmus of acceptability, if her body cannot accept your body then things are bleak for you. Later, other bodies will accept or reject you, but first you must surrender your cellular self to the XX universe of one woman at one time in her life.

I think it is significant that we notate the essential perpendicular relationship in mathematics as the XY axis, not P and Q, or T and L, when we consider our gender as XX and XY (factor out some reciprocal X to extract the XY axis). In fact, the Y shape intrigues as the masculine symbol, a branching (reaching) contour while X blocks, asserts itself edge to edge, a square rather than a wedge. It made me want to cry at the ridiculous beauty of life, there can be symmetry *but symmetry isn't required*. The child was knitting itself a body, poking out arm stubs and pooling organs in some individual version of the preferred configuration. Enough

Book II – Family. Life.

toes? Too many? Long legs, short body, medium head. Medium legs, medium body, little head. The bigger the fetus gets, the faster it can build itself. The genetic blueprint is set, now it is the general contractor who sets out to make the baby to spec., the biological tool belt of cell division and protein conversion gives you the beginnings of a body. Sometimes mechanical problems arise, perhaps the cord wraps around the ankle and reduces circulation to the foot enough to stunt it. You are laying your physical life's foundation. It's freaky that egg-sperm bombs mushroom into animate beings.

    I wasn't sure how harried men without enough time and money to go around had the luxury to think out the implications of pregnancy, maybe it was just as well they didn't contemplate bleak hard-fought futures – it was effort enough to slog forward in order not to fall backward. That's a valid strategy for getting your young to adulthood. The preferred strategy is to tilt odds in your collective favor, hunt harder, shelter better, prepare more. Working the road was soothing to me, I wasn't watching the vehicles, I was thinking of the people inside the vehicles, how it came to be that they were hurtling forward together at that moment, and why were those particular pedestrians there then too? I could finally see through situations and appreciate the circumstantial nature of outcome. A flat tire can aggravate you or it can kill you. Different factors like speed, location, conditions dictate the physical outcome of forces colliding. Human destiny lies in the choices of driver and passenger to challenge these odds. Wearing a seat belt will shift those numbers in your favor, why not look beyond your emotional response to being restrained and do the math? Ironically, the math also says certain stages of life manifest as rebellion, the terrible twos, mid-teens, early adulthood. Facts don't bother these age groups. They are not good extrapolaters. We cull our herd, we judge our calves, re-judge our adolescents, losing hold of those at the fringe of what we call success, those kids who are clinging to raggedy edges of what will and will not survive in the current conditions. Some break away and are gone. That's the cycle for all of us. Short life is still complete life. You are not alive, then you are, finally you are not. The serendipity of choice and chance control the on-off switch, pure will is not enough to sustain life, or to terminate it, because there must be a way of death… a way that kidney fails, a way that tree limb will snap *here* if you hit the tree *there* but *there* if *here*… the fact of the snap is the result of the hit but the nature of the snap depends on prevailing conditions. We're all actors, reactors, co-actors, pro-actors in circumstances within our influence while beyond our control.

    You get a second tier of statistical odds determined by the people who help the baby-you do the survival math until your brain grows enough to make choices for itself, these guardians decide whether to strap you in a baby carrier, a booster seat, a center shoulder belt, air-bags? By the time kids are self-loading passengers with other drivers, they should grasp the idea that car-makers are compelled to put seatbelts in cars because cars are unacceptable, inherently unsafe, without them. (And who would know better than the maker?) Wear the seat belt. We as a society mandate that. Flaunting this reveals itself in the real world as chipped teeth, broken jaws, cracked skulls, snapped necks. I see it all. I'm often chatty with accident victims who haven't been wearing seat belts, if they're in any condition to listen… I share the story of the girl who started out in the back seat yet punctured her throat with the dashboard Jesus… that's how hard and fast she flew forward when the car stopped. I tell the tale of the gear-shift imprint on the long-bone of what was left of a leg of a person who tumbled free in a roll-over over-roll. I can talk and work at the same time, dropping a conversational bomb (smothered driver whose face was pinned against her dog's corpse by the crumpled roof) then moving away to continue my job, turn back for another tidbit (there was this guy half-out the sunroof when his buddy's car flipped up against the trestle). The worst situations for me were people who set up infant projectiles, not giving the kid a fair chance by at the very least strapping them into a self-contained baby pod. These safety seats end up functioning as ejector seats if not fastened to the vehicle properly; still, that's better than lobbing the kid around without even a plastic shell to protect it.

I'm finding that I can see the end of my towing days ahead, I think there's a guy here in town who could be ready to buy me out in a few years, I see him headed this direction. He started out doing winter work, plowing mostly, but the lure of towing turned his head and soon he was taking lead on calls when I was gone, coming up with a better way to stow our gear, taking dispatchers on ride-alongs, making our business better. I was turning more towards the Kids Place as an outlet for my helping. It had been fun to kiss up against the lives of lots of strangers but it was more satisfying to apply my effort consistently. I liked the longer term perspective with this younger audience.

Kids are on loan, to their parents, to society, to whoever will supply their needs, they are not fully functional units yet, no matter what circumstance prevails at the moment. They aren't little grown-ups, and they don't stay kids forever. I thought about what I'd seen of Jared and Caroline's "late childhood" stages, pre-teens, new teens, middle teens, and I was getting a taste of Jared's end teens. At Kids Place we had tangible proof the Kids weren't "our" kids which only went to show that Jared and Caroline weren't ours either, not once they weren't little kids. "You used to be my baby" is so often misinterpreted as "You'll always be my baby." No… you won't. You always will have been the baby but babyhood is a brief interlude, a controlled on-ramp to the road of life into which you must merge, re-merge, picking your lane, setting your pace, it is a one-way highway as far as time is concerned, we weren't granted a physical rewind option (although we do possess a complex storage system for re-viewing what we think we've done). The baby learns to turn toward you, then crawl to you, toddle to you, walk to you, run to you, and ultimately to skip past you. Even our little baby floating in the womb devoted its energy to assembling a mono-pod [body] to live free of its mother, it had already been set loose from me the father. It was so easy to fall into the trap of thinking the baby was the meaning of your life. They are not, your commitment to being what they need (including being gone when they need you gone) is your accomplishment, how gracefully you move through the stages with them, including the ones where they seem to repudiate all that you are and ever will be. Parenting a teen takes some of the romance out of welcoming an infant, it turns out that contradiction vents the twined fear and hope that is pregnancy. If all Rose and I had to fill our time was staring at her expanding belly and thinking about what could go right and wrong with our baby inside, it would be like an inversion, a stagnation. Instead, we juggle our many elements, and the baby slips more easily into the mix.

Rose was particularly sensitive to scents mid-pregnancy so we sought out a soothing incense that pleased her. She taught me not to simply light a stick and set it in a holder, we slowly traced patterns into the air, wrote words of love in smoke, let the scent open up in the room. If it was dark, we did Dance of the Fireflies with the glowing tips. This was the kind of love I had hoped for, and worked for. Rose and I shared sensual feelings, finding our peculiar pleasures. We sometimes put our headphones on and listened to music while we made love, we didn't tell each other what was playing and this disconnect provided an endless variety of style adaptations. Once or twice we added blindfolds but we were left feeling too encapsulated, it was better when we could see each other even as the sounds piped into our ears precluded verbal communication.

In a sad way I understood I'd never love her the same as I loved her while she carried my baby for me, while she did what I couldn't do, and what nobody else had offered to do. She let my seed distend her stomach, fill her chest, burden her bladder. There's no way to thank her adequately but I try. I've always been solicitous in general but I reached a higher level while she marched forward in her current life – having the baby was the equivalent of going over the edge of the world, into the unknown, after a long voyage to get there. You can theorize all you want, it doesn't count until you are over the edge at which point there is no turning back. As my Grandmother told me, "A mother walks into the valley of death to bring a child to life." The genetic ticket is punched at conception (although it can degrade during replication), the clock starts ticking, and the Book of Souls adds another entry.

Book II – Family. Life.

    Our daughter was born one early evening in late May after a "rapid" seven-hour labor. The fact Rose already had birthed two kids weighed against the fact that was accomplished more than a dozen years ago… Rose had an epidural but that didn't block the muscle fatigue of her chest, shoulders and neck as she strained to power the birth (she said her toes were sore from clenching). It was an awesome display of physical power and I couldn't believe my dear darling wife faced and conquered that challenge with her modest body, it was a show of will that put any of my "competitions" to shame. Rose looked right in my eyes as the baby slipped free of her, willing me to see the light in her face as it glowed bright, brighter than it ever would again (unless she had another child). At baby's first high-pitched squeal, mother's eyes exploded with triumph, her lids dropped and she took several deep breaths; I almost fainted with my love of her. In these brief seconds, the doctor had stepped aside to inspect the baby and she looked over her shoulder at us. Rose didn't see it but I did, and it made me nervous, it wasn't but a moment or two more before the doctor turned to us and said, "Baby is fine, alert and breathing on her own. We'll bring her over in a minute." (Her!) Baby was toweled off, the brisk rubbing to help her (her!) circulation, while the delivery nurse helped Rose prepare to deliver the placenta. I didn't know what I was supposed to be doing so I concentrated on keeping my feet on the floor. I was the father of a daughter, my girl had arrived!

    Eileen Ruby Clover arrived and nothing would ever be the same.

    Mrs. D had never been comfortable with the idea of being a baby nurse, she envisioned herself much more like a Great Aunt, so we had agreed to look for a nanny; more precisely, two part-time nannies. Rose wanted help from after breakfast to after lunch, and after dinner to bedtime, plus weekends and extra hours as mutually agreed, offering one week off each month while Rose and Eileen worked at the Kids' Place. We had the luxury to engage household help yet we hesitated, nobody who applied seemed right. What we finally realized was that we really wanted a new mom to help us, and for the baby of that mom to be part of the team. Baby Eileen was going to be living in a house full of big people, we thought she would benefit from having another little person around. We were also aware that the job could be an important resource for that mom: income, companionship, work experience. We were looking for a responsible person, preferably with some practical life experience (nurse? life guard?). Like all things connected with Eileen, we jumped off the ordinary.

Rose suspected, like the doctor, that the tiny girl with the hooded eyes and low ears was the result of a DNA knitting error, and instead of 46 chromosomes, she had 47. There are 23 pairs to match up and if her 21st "pair" was a "trio", she was built with the Down Syndrome design. What delayed the diagnosis was the fact Eileen was a member of an even smaller subset, where only a portion of the 21st pairs are trios, they call this variation "mosaic". Down Syndrome manifests in l of 800 births, and the mosaic variety represents only about 3% of that small population. It's a matter of degree, they talk about percentages of mosaicism – what did that mean to my little girl? She was a Down Syndrome kid but she wasn't. Her ears were small and low set, she had a gap between her big toe and the rest of her toes, she had a single crease on her palm… but you had to look close to notice. She was slightly round-faced, her neck wasn't long, her pinky bent in the middle (the ordinary finger has three segments but these pinkies have two). I wouldn't see those things until later, and then I would stop seeing them like a symptom checklist. I saw my daughter, Eileen, in all her beauty and brattiness, working at making a life for herself, fighting to wear a certain pink shirt, tasting the dog food so she could growl to Sovereign about its flavor… all of this makes up my honey-pie.

Rose told me in the delivery room, before we joined the kids waiting to see us and meet their sister, that she wanted me to understand that Eileen was fine, she was healthy, she was different, and we were excellently positioned to help her be herself. The way we would for any kid. I was stunned, screw the science, I knew I had a lot to learn, but I already knew I loved that baby, Eileen. Eileen Ruby. I was proud to be the parent of that baby. Rose's first concern was for Eileen, she wanted her presented fairly from the get-go. The tests we declined during the pregnancy were now going to be done directly on the baby to quantify the percentage of chromosomal involvement. Was it 3 good splits of 4 (25% involved)? Was it 7 good splits of 8 (12.5% involved)? It was a number calculated by stacking the 21st pairs against the 21st trios. It weighted the probability that little Eileen would lag behind her peers, and never quite catch up, perhaps she could be expected to have a sheltered job, participate in social outings, play sports, date and maybe marry. She probably wouldn't have a child. All of this knots up in my head, what I know now and that one searing moment of realization that my kid had a tougher-than-usual road ahead.

I was in agreement with Rose that we wouldn't discuss newborn Eileen's possible chromosome counting error with others until we understood the extent of it, after we had time to consider what we needed to do beyond all the things we already planned to do with a new baby. Our daughter had an impish quality to her face that, in time, would seem inappropriate but it was darling on an infant. Jared would hold her only when she was asleep, his love expressed by his fear of making a mistake with her. Caroline cuddled Eileen so naturally we could see that she was going to be her sister's defender, running interference. The kids were responding to Eileen's tiny size, there was nothing to tip them off that complications might lie ahead. Heart… eyes… ears… as parents we knew where to look but had to wait to see. She was a typical newborn sleeping most of the time, her eyes weren't expected to focus, she turned toward sudden noises, she cried in high little yelps (small lungs), and the tip of her tongue showed when she was asleep. I wish I could make you see how sweet she was, and how much I would have missed in life if I didn't meet this exact specific baby girl. It came to me that this was what Rose had been telling me when she declined the genetic screening, that the baby deserved to live and die unmolested by our selfish wish to avoid anxiety. If someone told me about mosaic Down Syndrome I would have thought I understood that this was the dark line of choice associated with pregnancy screening, some of the fetuses will not live, most will, and some are proceeding with various wounds in their weave. This distinct cellular structure did not mean the person was not viable. Viability proved itself. Eileen's arrived.

Trisomy 21 is the tiniest error that magnifies itself into various cell lines and insidiously expresses itself within certain known patterns. We can conjure up a symbolic face for Down Syndrome, they are of such a strongly-marked tribe that we see these features stamped on western and eastern people, on the dark and the light. Observing this syndrome overrides our gender and race categories, these are people made with a different blueprint. In a way they exist at a different rate of consumption. Everything is thicker and slower, the speech comes late, growth is protracted. The idea they are lesser is inaccurate, they are distinct. They require accommodation to pass through the big busy world of the majority, they are intent on their simpler but no less valuable goals. The process of dressing and catching a bus can occupy the available capacity of a person, they do it the same way every day or they would forget how to do it. Most of us dash through these maintenance tasks without thinking but there are those who have to stop and remember how to button every button. They are comforted when they can do it. In some ways, their inefficient retrieval of memory is what hampers them when measured by our go-go standards. They do not make rapid associations between the past and the future. (Maybe it is because the "now" looms so large that the future seems far away.) It is like watching a slow-growing tree make its tough wood. Changing the basic configuration of one gene pair out of twenty-three determines the most complicated systems of the human. Task-orientation rather than big-picture thinking is a method, it is not a "value", both are modes of self-aware behavior.

Rose and I felt each other's stormy dreams when Eileen first came home and we knew, deep inside, we were battling to interpret our own reactions to an altered configuration of family, cleaning out unrealistic expectations, adjusting our lenses. It is the same sort of vivid imagery that haunts grief dreams except for us there was the counterbalance of a new future, and we struggled individually with the idea of parenting a kid with special needs. We were looking at an elongated childhood and from our mature vantage that made the need to have plans for her in place as soon as possible. Even with the best of luck, our little Eileen was going to need security after we were dead. We were trying to provide cushions for Jared and Caroline but in truth they were well set-up for success and could be expected to sustain themselves by their mid-twenties, with or without us. When considering Eileen, we had to retain the responsibility for filling the gap so she could participate in the real world all her life. We could subsidize an apartment, cover medical/dental insurance, arrange for qualified home health care workers to the extent required, augment her earnings from a simple job… this was the optimistic plan – it was possible she might need sheltered care all her life. So much depended on the exact number of trios at position 21, tossed against the strength of her spirit. The Down Syndrome genetic inaccuracy is that a certain pair of chromosomes splits and becomes three (or translocate). Every subsequent split repeats the error. In Mosaic Down Syndrome, the error is not made at the initial cell division but later… perhaps when two cells become four, or when four become eight. Pinpointing the basis of replication error through cell testing determines the ratio of involvement… if seven of eight split into pairs and one into a trio, then on the next split there will be two trio and fourteen pair; then four trio and twenty-eight pair… eight trio and fifty-six pair…. pairs will be in the majority. Even if the error is delayed from first to second split, it halves the genetic impact. But not all Down Syndrome kids are alike, no matter their genetic equation. When we talk about predicting the outcome of a genetic legacy, we have to allow for the complexity of individual accomplishment – it is statistically true that MDS has less visible effects than DS, but it's always a matter of individuality. What would become of Eileen Ruby Clover?

Jared spent two weeks in the middle of the summer after Eileen was born helping me re-roof, scrape and paint the shore house. He was going to be a senior in high school, he was readying his launch pad to leave us, and Rose worried about him. I figured he'd do OK, he knew how to tuck and roll. He was a good kid with a sharp eye. He felt like talking, so I listened.

"It's like this, Jerry. About Eileen. I'm just saying, I'm going to be gone to college before she's even a person. She's going to think I'm a giant, I don't feel like we're going to have any kind of way to relate to each other."

"You need to start earlier, and work harder, to get her to notice you. You *are* a giant and you're going to be a beacon for her."

"Like, I'm her protector, when you guys die, right? No offense, but, I mean... it's like that, right?"

"Oh, yeah. Always has been. You do the same thing for Caroline, you started it instinctively, don't let your growing-up brain get in the way of that. You're Eileen's brother, perhaps the only one she'll ever have."

"Perhaps? You're going to have more kids?"

"We didn't know we were going to have this one."

"You can borrow my health book if you need information about that. But, what I was saying was, I know you've done the money stuff. But what will she want?"

"She'll let us know. Don't work too hard trying to figure out her limitations, Jared. She will always need her brother to listen and watch, you'll know what's right."

"Yeah, I mean, what do we really know about how things are going to turn out? Mom told me to quit acting like Eileen is a science experiment. It's like, hearing that puts things into proper perspective. What am I worried about? She's my sister, she's my sister's sister. I'm doubled in."

"Nice."

"And that half-brother thing, that's just clumsy, man. She isn't my father's kid but then neither am I, I'm my mother's kid and so is she. It's like, I'm giving her my mother, in a way. And it's cool she's got a real dad."

"We're a good team, you're a big player for us."

"Marquee!"

"Hardeen, The Next Generation."

"Got to be better because we couldn't be worse."

"Youch. Little tough on us forefathers."

Book II – Family. Life.

"My dad's a jerk. You never even knew your dad. How do you know you can do this 'dad' stuff?"

"I said I would so I will."

There was a little girl named Caroline and she had a heart of gold, spun gold, she wasn't solid in the way that some people are. Caroline had the hardest experience as a child because there was nobody backing up her mother. Starlight had Grandma, Grandma had Carl, Jared's dad had been with Rose for the first few years… but toddler Caroline only had a Mommy grownup who she had to share with her brother. Her brother wasn't much help to her when she was very young because he was so young himself. He didn't hurt her, which helped, because this little girl could get all tangled up in her thoughts and didn't erect much of a defensive perimeter. She appeared absent-minded; it was a fact her mind wandered and she willingly meandered along with it. She didn't find satisfaction in the physical world as an infant, her mother was doing her best but it simply wasn't enough: her diapers were left on a little too long, her meals were lukewarm, there was a shortage of stimulation, so she dove inward. She more than made up for it later, soaking in the real value of happiness as her life improved after Rose finished nursing school and then met my grandmother, Mrs. Eileen. Caroline *felt* the improvement, she had softer sheets and better shoes and satisfying food. She was thrilled to welcome a little sister to the family, she knew she had to pay attention to Eileen in a way she'd never done with the rest of us, we had been dismissed from her consideration – not unkindly even if deliberately – she had been the baby, with less responsibility. Now she had to turn around and look after somebody else. Eileen's arrival gave Caroline a way to work through her feelings about her own babyhood. She could see how much *comfort* I would add (as dad) to the baby's world, how Eileen's bed would be snug and her windows clean and her planetarium mobile safety-hung out of reach. I had always helped with the housework, the homework, the yard work, I was protective of Rose and didn't merely insist she relax, I enabled her to relax. Caroline, daughter of a pregnant mother, saw advantage in that.

Eileen meant something different to each of us, but we felt a common challenge to make the right moves with her and for her. To pretend she wouldn't have a specific range of ability wasn't going to help any more than dismissing what intelligence she did have as insufficient. She could and would evolve, that's one definition of being alive… to learn from experience, to shape your behavior to enhance your survival. And she wasn't the only one evolving. Rose and I made careful love after Eileen arrived, re-doubling the contraception, because we weren't even ready to discuss the idea of another child which we had to do before we would ever discuss sterilization (although I felt we would both have to agree to be sterilized, or neither, it was a statement as much of our marriage as of our individuality, in the sense one should not unilaterally impose or deny a parenting choice of the other).

I understood that Rose wanted Eileen to be trusted to embrace her own life, to reach for what she wanted. She wanted that for all of us, and I saw more clearly how my wife went about engineering that. She had Mrs. D in thrall, the neighbors waved her over, everybody included her, and I was proud she incorporated me with her.

"It's science, Jared. Not mind control."

"Why does everything have to be your way, Mother?"

"In my house, it's my way. I'm looking at your room from a health standpoint. Balled up wet towels in your closet are a problem for me. The carpet gets damp. You introduce bacteria not usually found on the closet floor. There's a hamper in your room, you can even keep the lid open, paint a target on it… I want the wet and dirty clothes to go there. Just there and right there. That's all. I need things done that way and I've made it easy for you to do."

"Fine. Have it your way. I agree stinky clothes go in the hamper."

"The other part of the agreement? Clothes discarded on the floor are not yours any more. They are tossed away."

"What?"

"I am going to let you make choices. Things you want to ever wear again in your life are either put away or put in the hamper. I'm too busy to argue with you time and time again. I've simplified it for you. A-B-C. Put away, or in the hamper, or gone."

"Where will they go?"

"They'll just be gone."

"What if you took them but I could earn them back?"

"Then they wouldn't be gone, would they? I'd just be picking them up and storing them for you to be redeemed at your convenience. I don't have that time for that."

"All right, already."

"You're wearing me down having to remind you of these basic courtesies. Quit wasting my time, and take charge of yourself."

"I get it, Mom… I'm sorry."

"Sorry's easy to say, Jared. I'm counting on you to step up here, and help me out. I need to know you 'get it', no joke. I'm almost forty and have a baby. You can't leave screwdrivers laying around, you have to shut the cupboards. This family needs to baby-proof the house, and you have to help."

"I know that. Really. I get it, about you being so old and having a kid."

The poker games at the shore have a fresh twist now that we've added a female player; Gwendy is the new owner of the Shores Chores agency. Chores is the successful entrepreneurial effort started by my old girlfriend Reed who has since adopted some kids and chose life in the City. We neither of us saw our respective futures back then, yet Reed and I each ended up happy after we broke up, something we hoped for each other (and for ourselves), and by doing that we transcended beyond the intimacy of sex to the prize of affection. We don't have any reason to be jealous or cause jealousy – it's hard to explain if you don't believe that even good sex can be put away and contained when circumstances change.

What I saw was that Gwendy was the polar opposite of Reed in every way except running a chores agency… they both got the work done at a profit through repeat customers. Off-hours, Gwendy straddled a cut-down Harley, strapped on a helmet, zipped up her leathers and rode the road. She was a loner most of the time so her participation in the poker nights gave her a foothold with the local merchants. She wasn't anybody's idea of a "target" for innuendo, she didn't play that. The closest eye couldn't decide if she was hetero, lesbo, bi- or asexual… but the clearer message was not to waste your time trying to figure it out since you had no reason to know. Given the small population of the town, we'd always kept the card game conversations to sports, weather, vehicles and other quasi-logical topics. We noted only the major events that changed the town's landscape and appeared in our local paper: a death, a divorce, a new baby, a second spouse… and maybe we lifted our eyebrows at the timing… but there was nothing to be gained by opining out loud about our neighbors because words like that twirl in the wind and can be thrown back at you.

Gwendy especially liked competitive games, it wasn't the card playing so much as the skirmishing, every hand affected by the order of the players, the draw of the cards, each new deal meant another chance to clash. She wasn't combative, she put herself into a head-to-head situation with others because she, the same as the rest of us at this particular table, liked to spar. Jabs and feints, raises and bluffs, within the possibilities of fifty-two cards in five pair of hands. Good player, Gwendy. Fast with the math, easy with the odds, it was entertaining to sit in a game with her.

We'd never been a particularly raunchy bunch before she joined us; again, it seemed we knew we'd be seeing each other around town and didn't want to set our standards too low. There were ways to be good neighbors and some of that was keeping your distance.

Rose was the one who let me see that Gwendy would fit perfect with the guys; it wasn't anything she said, it was the fact that she herself would never have wanted to join us. Rose wasn't a card player, she didn't find it fun to argue unanswerable questions. Just suppose, for instance, there was a test that could tell you the date you were going to die, would you take that test? If you did, would you tell anybody else the answer? If you

Book II – Family. Life.

told them an answer, would it be the true answer? Rose wouldn't accept the premise because there wasn't such a machine so the rest of the dialog was nonsense to her. Gwendy, on the other hand, understood that such conversations were moral explorations, ways to get to know a person's method of thinking and system of signals. Once I got to know her that way, I could see how she'd fit in at the games. It wasn't even such a big deal when I suggested letting a girl in the club house, it was only temporary! Gus was going to spend the fall in Virginia, helping his brother settle into a "retirement village". Gus was adamant that he was coming back to the game, that we shouldn't believe him if he called and said he wanted to stay there. If he said he found it "relaxing", that would be the code for alerting us he was trapped on the manicured streets, in which case we were to mount a rescue. We needed a temporary fifth in his absence, and Gwendy was willing to take the chair on that basis. No commitment on either side.

In a way, we were the local Better Business Bureau, each of us had a commercial enterprise of one kind or another so it was important to know the pulse of our community, and just as important you spoke up when you saw need for improvement. We probably swayed a few town elections, and surely got the recycling initiative going, but that was a by-product of our primary purpose which was to relax in familiar company. Chill. We were set for odd-date Thursdays. Some of us played in other games but none of us played each other anywhere else. It was a deliberate decision, made early on, not to unbalance the table by creating coalitions. We had a private circle, and it was as fair as it reasonably could be. There was no penalty for missing a game because none of us would skip if we didn't have to. Bringing in Gwendy was tantamount to inviting her to consider herself an authorized sub, she could be called upon by any of us (after Gus got back) to fill the table.

I intercepted Jared on his way into the house after school one day, told him to drop his books and get ready for a ride. To him that meant clean socks and fresh shoes. He already dressed in layers so he was ready for just about any turn of weather. He was seventeen and found me a tolerable sports buddy but otherwise dismissed me as too old to "get it". We bonded within the universe of the NBA. I'd grown up watching baseball on TV but gained an appreciation for basketball because he liked it so much. He'd spout statistics at me, he was a student of the game. Jared took his sports stars seriously; they were being given the world to do a fun job and he thought slacking was low-class. In that sense, he judged every player's effort (considering the amount of talent) and demonstrated his own good sense of character.

When he asked where we were going on our ride, I said, we're going to see a guy downtown. It was an odd trip for after school and he flashed over to wary. What guy? Why him and me? He was a careful kid and I exploited a bit of that to sharpen his feelings. I let him pick the radio stations (!) but I retained control of the volume during the jockeying through rush hour traffic clogged by the migration of NBA fans to a playoff game. I asked him to roll down his window and watch for a big guy wearing a brown jacket and black jeans. He'd have a sign like all the "got ticket" and "need ticket" merchants surrounding the arena but his target sign would say "Jared". We spotted the guy in plenty of time for me to roll to the curb (I'd known all along exactly where we'd meet him). Jared sat very still, placed as he was between me and a massive man at the passenger window who was handing me a white envelope, barreling out salutations to me and shaking Jared's hand (which I suspect was already shaking). I pulled into the garage attached to the arena and had Jared pull a parking pass out of the envelope, it said "Courtside-Reserved". We parked in a VIP spot and walked down a ramp to tables of free food and beverages, *onto the actual basketball court* and crossed to our seats, second row courtside, seats 9-10 so we're practically parallel to the hoop, on the floor, on the floor!

Jared was agog, balancing a giant cookie, popcorn, hotdog, water and program as we walked over TV cables and around the key to our impossibly wonderful seats. I knew I had absolutely blown his brain out the back of his head. Our team was up 3-1 in a best of seven series. This means they only had to win one of the final three games to proceed to the next round… but any one they won won the series. It would be great to do it tonight but if they didn't it was not a disaster. This game was golden; it was all about the play.

Jared had been to a few games over the years, in the cheap seats, with us or with his friends, so he knew his way around the public arena, this area was much more exclusive. We were within eight feet of the court; there was the green border on the floor marking out of bounds, Row AA of seats then our BB-9 and BB-10. The crowd was loud, the game was tight, the lead see-sawed until the end, up two, down four, up nine, down six… it was so *fast* and so *furious* and what looked like "touches" on TV were jabs and pressure up close. The dancers were very bouncy, the mascot was an athlete too. There is a contagious glee when an event works as hoped, when a scene is set, a song is sung, a talent shown. There's smugness in the crowd because they are there, they are spectating, they are more involved than the TV fans, they are dressed up and gathered for a common cause, even if done in a multitude of styles.

A nattily-dressed old couple toddled into front row seats, a young family, a mix of genders and ages, but still it was the province of active males, they expressed their hunting skill by scoring tickets, they got the good territory on the tundra… I looked enough like one of them to blend as far as outsiders were concerned, but the die-hard fans knew we were guests of someone like them. It was obvious Jared was a true believer so I got an extra dose of tolerance. Inevitably, the tipsy gal at the front corner toppled her beer cup, luckily it happened in between the halves. Jared rolled his eyes at me, didn't the woman know she was in a civic temple? I was able to surrender to the experience completely, not having planned more than an hour in advance (when I got a call from my big friend he churned game tickets for pocket money, he'd pick up a pair of tickets for $150 pre-season and sell for $400 if it turns out to be a hot game, a set for $300 out for $410… dealing to keep one good seat for himself.) I knew he was aware I had a teenage stepson and that the tickets were as much a pay-back to me as a gift to Jared. I could have made the effort to buy tickets for any game but we simply didn't think that way, we planned to watch each game on TV together, benefiting from the replays and audible commentary. Instead, unexpectedly, we were part of the thunder of fans who squeezed into tight chairs in close rows then jumped up, waved, whistled, clapped before settling back down. You experience the game surrounded by others. Courtside puts it to scale, the players are rough and ready, fleet footed, graceful in the air. In between all that they mill around in their tall richness and wait for play to resume. Statisticians may break numbers by the year but these guys face each other over many years, in various combinations, they KNOW each other and they KNOW how to play each other. That's something that I had missed through the screen. It made logical sense but seeing it close up rang emotionally.

Jared checked the half-time stat sheet distributed down the row like school papers, take one and pass them on... I separated the various elements of the arena, the lighted signs, the flashing ads, the televised version in a jumbo screen above, tiers of seats, all tilted toward the court where camera crews duck-walked and diplomats (ushers) roamed. A uniformed cop watched the crowd from our corner, his back to the game, scanning the stands, one of four cops bottle-stopping access to the corners of the court. He could tell the way the game was going by watching the watchers, listening to their cheers and groans, the over-arch announcer detailing the play; cops weren't there to see the game.

Eileen was a slow-burning ember, delicate and easily overlooked. She was alert to stimuli but took her own sweet time processing it. She heard the door to the nursery snick open then you could see the construction of her response. She froze and put all her energy on stringing together the sequence: notice, decide, act. It was the matter of a slow beat, thoughts all happened in the right order but gradually. I know I was looking for things like that, ways to watch her mind work. It helped I hadn't ever known another infant, Rose had clearer expectations and more concrete concerns. I was heartened by watching my little girl learn, it seemed to me I could see ahead to her having fun, being excited, looking up at the stars... that's all I wanted for any kid, to have the future. Was it fair that she had a genetic anomaly? Fair to her? Fair to us? Fair that she didn't

Book II – Family. Life.

get something even more challenging? Would it be luckier to be a bright child born to an abusive family? These are the things you take on faith, you have the instinct that new life is precious; none of us should diminish the value of its impossibility to be replaced.

We were working with a sensory therapist so that Eileen was given a rich infancy. It made sense that the sooner she was engaged in multi-sensory environments the more easily she'd adapt to the challenges ahead of her. We played music with simple rhythms, changed the color of the light in the room by selecting one of four primary-color window shades to tint the white walls. We used spices and herbs to scent the air. We talked to her, sometimes from a short distance, so we were just sound, sometimes we locked eyes up close and said her name and smiled at her, lifting her cheeks with our fingertips so she *felt* the smile. We were careful to integrate this directed learning with good old-fashioned babying, we snuggled and hugged her, the kids took turns cranked back in the recliner balancing their baby sister on their laps. It wasn't hard to love Eileen.

Mrs. D. told me one night how lucky Eileen was to be born in the United States in the new millennium, she remembered her own youth when "defectives" didn't survive the harsh social realignment, they were easily spotted and eliminated by arrogant elitists. The Nazis' collective belief they were fit to choose the fate of others made them a danger to themselves. They couldn't see the impact of their genocide in the larger picture, they had small-focus need to dominate their immediate environment… they are dismissed in history as nutballs and losers for thinking they were a Master Race. Mrs. D. was hitting her seventies in good stride, not traveling alone any more, but otherwise living as she always had, looking for a good deal she could pass on to a satisfied customer. She met with Rose and her attorney to lay out the details of her estate in the event of her death, and we showed her the arrangements we'd made for her in the event of ours.

The Wrath of Rose fell upon Jared and Jared was sorely tested, oh, woe and pain rained down on the boy who had acted the fool, and, worse, lied when caught. There weren't many things that could blow Rose's gasket but underage drinking did it. She loathed alcohol as an excuse for bad behavior, it was tantamount to blindfolding yourself then expecting to be forgiven for stumbling into other people. Jared was eighteen, it was tough for me to agree with her that him having a few beers signaled the end of civilization (I had my own guilty memories of foolishness at that age). Then I thought of the smashed kids I saw on the road and changed my mind. It wasn't only that Jared got a little drunk, but that he was with people who might be quite a bit drunker than he was. Impairing your own judgment when in the company of impaired people really shifts the odds that trouble will result. Besides, it wasn't a matter of opinion but of law: he was underage. Period.

The lying part was more of an evasion, an act of omission. I could see that flicker of sneaky calculation before he answered his mother's question about where he had been Friday night. I almost winced, because if I caught it then it was a red flag to his mother. He had compounded a mistake into a deliberate breach of her trust, and it was going to cost him.

He thought he could bluff toughness, not a good idea with a woman like Rose. She might seem to be the cool clinician and superb organizer but those were only things she *did*, what she *was* was true. She didn't have to menace him with violence, or make empty threats. She looked him right in the face and let him see her disappointment, not shielding it like she would for a younger child caught in some transgression. He wanted to have the rights of an adult, then he could handle the heat of an adult reaction. She wasn't only his mother talking to him, she was at full strength, direct and specific. He'd be on restriction, with an earlier curfew, not to punish him but because he didn't deserve better than that. He would need to earn back privileges, but he was told she wouldn't be taking applications to advance for at least a month. He was in the doghouse and it was good he could see that. He still cared enough to be rattled by her fury. They had argued in the past but he had never crossed the line like he did by lying to her about something this important.

Book II – Family. Life.

It was a turning point in their relationship, he was making choices that she couldn't cushion.

His silly-drunk buddies had dropped him off then run into a parked car about a mile away. It wasn't a horrible wreck... they were going slow, belted in. Jared had already left the car at the time of the accident, his name came up in the investigation as the last stop before the crash, the reason they were going that direction on that street at that time. We got a heads-up call from the cops the next morning, it was too late to take Jared's blood to test for alcohol. They just wanted us to know that they considered this his only warning. There wouldn't be a lot of tolerance for having to meet him in person over some future incident.

"I said it was stupid, Mother. I did a bad thing. I won't drink again."

"It isn't what you did, Jared... it's how you handled your choices. If you want to try drinking, don't mix it with driving. If you want to tempt fate, don't involve innocent people. If you can't decide what's right to do, ask yourself what Eli would tell you to do."

"That's not fair."

"Your friend being dead isn't fair. Don't do things you don't want to live with. Or die for."

"I get it, Mom."

"I know you think you do. You don't have to be perfect but you better get better at making choices because these count, Jared. You're playing for keeps now."

Starlight had reduced her contact even further, after we bridged my grandmother's death it turned out we had little in common. She didn't know me, I didn't know her. Her own grandchild was of no particular interest to her, she was more concerned with the Universal Ideas of Existence in Harmonious Rapture than the tendril on a family tree she had pruned herself from. I reviewed her health plans, made sure we were listed as emergency contacts on the few forms she agreed to file with The Man, and took her out to dinner in the fall each year, we were one stop on her annual trek to revisit places of significance in her life. She drove the roads a little slower as time passed, for better or worse she was settled in her ashram, and still some little spark got her on the move.

She did ask me if maybe some acid she took before I was born might be one cause for Eileen's situation. I told her everything about her did root in Eileen's life, as well as my own, and her mother's, matched by the contribution of Rose, and on and on, up and down the genetic chain. We wore faces shaped by the people in our blood line. I pointed out Down Syndrome is a known defect that predated Timothy Leary's psychedelic gospel. Starlight had an identical lack of responsibility for the fact Eileen had a good home, top-rate insurance, and committed sponsors. This was the sort of thing that used to turn me off about Starlight, everything was analyzed with her at the center, it was very much an "I" reference point. She was quick to dodge blame, and her question about being responsible was not to share the burden, only to calculate its potential size in order to sidestep it. She didn't realize that nobody was to "blame" for Eileen.

I understood that people meeting our daughter didn't know what to say, or how to say it… they wanted to say things like she was precious in spite of this, um, flaw; it didn't seem right to say it was a shame… they were reacting to the presumably limited potential of my child. She was singled out as incomplete, when in fact we are all just snippets stitched together to make one person's one life and each of those has various potential. People's reaction to Eileen was stronger than it would have been to a more conventional child, still I knew all kids are judged on appearance and outward suitability long before they are assessed for their inner qualities. This was a little girl who wouldn't ever pass a nasty chain letter although she'd be mentioned, "{Insert name here} is so dorky not even Eileen understands her." She wouldn't join a gang, hire a hit man, drive drunk. She wasn't going to be an angel even if she had little potential as an effective criminal. We had to teach her to be honest, true and hard-working. Just like the other kids.

"It ain't coming out of there in one piece."
"A crane could do it."

"You'd have to top the tree; I say we get in a boom and start cutting it up."

"It's a car, not a kite. We can't just cut it into four easy pieces and let it drop. You can't cut the gas line."

"We could take off the doors and the roof, the hood, the tires. Reduce the weight then maybe we could winch it out of there."

"Any word on the driver?"

"He's alive, last I heard. Flipped over the guard rail, landed high in the tree, engine pointing down. A miracle, really, the car didn't keep going right through it."

"Heart attack?"

"Maybe stroke... witnesses say he slumped at the wheel and drove straight off the curve, no skid marks. Went airborne. Paramedics say his heart is strong."

"When did he fall out of the car?"

"Not sure. He was still in the car when it hit, yet he ended up on the ground. They can see where he fell through the branches. He might have been disoriented and unfastened his seat belt which would have been his only support when he was upside down; I heard he's pretty banged up."

"I want to die in my sleep."

"I can't think of a good way to go...."

"Can think of plenty of bad ones..."

Bad. Bad bad. Ugly sites where people misjudged their machines and/or themselves resulting in the clash of distinct momentums. Particle A is headed a certain way at a certain speed while Particle B heads opposite and slower while Particle C runs perpendicular and faster. At what points, if any, will they converge?

It isn't all car wrecks. It's a guy trapped under an engine in his barn and me closest with a winch; it's a kid in a well and I can provide a generator, heavy-duty tools, ideas, and I can freeze when I hear them talk about a recovery rather than a rescue. One word difference. The quick and the dead. The shore involves me in the community because I asked them to do so. I hung up a sign with my name and stayed in the towing business, extending my concept of family through the folks gathered in this quiet spot. In the city, things were tighter, more compressed, the calendar was full, somebody was always on their way somewhere, and I could not find the time to care so much about the doings of others. Bingo. Another burst of Starlight... she was a communal person, she gave what she could to get what she needed. The component tasks of belonging were fine with her, she'd do her required amount of chores, kick in cash, follow the spirit of exchange. She just didn't want to be asked to monitor the mechanics of the real world, she liked to meditate on Life's Forces, not remit quarterly estimated payments to the Tax Bandits.

Rose and I are the opposite of my vagabond mother, we're fee payers and guideline abiders. We conform in the public ways so we can stay unique in our private life. We outright own the places we live, our names don't appear on police blotters, we are alike in the sense of earning freedom, balancing our own equations, paying attention to the feelings of others around us to avoid agitating them. Bureaucrats can make deadly enemies. We worked for a relaxed lifestyle, no bill collectors, no faulty cars, we were frugal with our good fortune so that our multi-sited lifestyle was possible.

We realized that Eileen was going to need to settle into a school somewhere, her best chance of sustained progress was to provide a constant environment, one that held to an overall philosophy from pre-school to kindergarten, to elementary, to middle, to high, to higher still. To do that, we had to decide if Eileen was best served in the city. We could see that the shore was an enrichment place already, rules relaxed, the life beat was stronger. We decided to preserve it as a hide-away. Her school was going to be one of structured improvisation, literally teaching her to think, rewarding her for thinking, giving her an appreciation for her own options in a situation. We thought of it as feathering her with knowledge, creating substance from wisps.

She had the opportunity to hook into services down at the Kids Place, we gave that a lot of thought. In the end, we realized our family life had always been in the city and the Kids Place was where we worked at the moment. Eileen would benefit from the mix of kids in the larger city programs, allowing her to place a multi-layered context around herself. She, too, had to learn to be sensitive to others of differing ability.

We picked a school, after all was said and done, because they had a buddy program. Each year all kids were assigned a school buddy, one grade older, a successful graduate of the challenge now facing each of them (who was in turn being buddied by an older student...). Their daily meeting was a "mixed" session with all ages and program levels: advanced, standard, specialized – the opposite of efficiency. In most other classes, subgroups in each grade addressed either end of the bell curve that is student achievement. The standard kids swelled the center while the very dim and very bright bracketed them. "Mainstreaming" was the buzz word for the lesson dynamics, we were overwhelmed with educational theory, in practice the buddy program showed us a culture of cooperation. We believed, a little bit, in Go Along to Get Along, ride the flow, work the odds, benefit from the experience of others. We didn't mean to surrender your standards, it meant you watched for bumps in the road and steered around them.

Having decided that, we then had to figure out how to provide continuity at home for Eileen when it happened that both Rose and I would be on the road, the part-time nannies couldn't be expected to change jobs. Mrs. D was definitely settled in the family as a Great Aunt. It was Caroline who asked why we didn't build on space for a live-along house manager. Why didn't we? We could offer a semi-detached apartment, Caroline suggested a breezeway lined with leaded stained glass – a passage between environments.

Brilliant! We decided that time was money in this case, so we hired a construction team to work in over-drive on a steep bonus scale for early completion. We didn't waste time daydreaming about the addition, we put it together from the most standard of modern conveniences; we weren't building it on the cheap, all the rooms had moldings and trim, grounded outlets, the windows were double-glass. We weren't sure who might live there over the years so we kept everything simple, providing a backdrop to any number of configurations. We knew we wanted the house manager to have a child or two, in addition to education and experience with early childhood development. This was not going to eliminate the jobs done by our two part-time nannies, we thought it was a good investment of our money to finance the lives of three deserving parents in return for Eileen's focus on school. It did wonders for household maintenance to have someone on-site. We operated like a relay team, some of us were sprinters and others marathoners, everybody had opportunity to contribute. We thought this was the model for any therapeutic environment, a mix of full-timers and part-timers, deepening perspective, multiplying opportunities for interaction. This experience helped us re-think the staffing at the Kids Place, spreading the wealth of employment and opportunity to a larger pool, splitting some jobs even if it doubled our benefit load, because we had two deserving candidates. We didn't forget the value of constancy, even in a limited role. Scenarios abound as do candidates to enact them. Our window-washer came once a week, alternating outside and inside. The Kids Place was founded on the concept of maintenance. Once you got going, you wanted to stay going. We all got used to each other, it was routine, and kids could feel the connection. Wednesday Windows. It was also a way to get a savvy adult into the kids' room on a regular basis. He was part fire-inspector and part Sunshine Bringer. A vendor with access to the site like that is checked and re-checked, and still we all watch each other. It's instinctive, protect the lambs.

Eileen was a slow, deliberate lamb. Ideas did not pop for her, they slowly burbled to the surface, one slow rise then another. I imagined her thought-pipes as congested (constricted). She and I spent time outside, in all kinds of weather, experiencing the wonder of rain and the fear of thunder, outside was huge for her, because she mastered it so slowly. Walking her back and forth, around the same old neighborhood, sometimes overstimulated her... too much information and her thoughts gridlocked. We took her downtown even if it made her fussy. Too much input paralyzed her output but by exposing her to this in measured doses she learned to cope. We introduced her to daily life, at the snail's pace she preferred.

Book II – Family. Life.

A toddler will eventually dash into various rooms in their house, Eileen stopped at every doorway before deciding to enter or not. If she entered a room, she stopped at the next intersection and made another decision… leave the room or stay in it. She wouldn't have peace in her home until she was much older, almost six. Years and years after her age-mates were at ease in their environment, Eileen moved warily. Jared noticed that she looked like she was always waiting to be startled, that was very observant of him because it put into words the reality that ordinary things did surprise her. The phone shrieked, the clock bonged, the dryer buzzed when it was finished. The reverse of this is that everything was fresh for Eileen, she always liked the toast popping up, every single time. It was her first word: tosz!

 I got hooked up with a tow-guy in the neighboring county, his wife got a dream job a thousand miles away and he thought it was a chance for a new life. He'd established his business fine; however, over time, the sadness of road accidents had overtaken him. Ten silly fender-benders don't wipe away a single head-on. He was going to roll what I paid him into an auto-parts franchise with his brother. I suddenly had twice as many people on the towing payroll, and three trucks instead of one. I wanted the lessons I learned from my old business to be stamped on the new one. It would be worry enough running an organized business, I couldn't tolerate a cranky crew or sloppy work. I was going to need a shop foreman, and that person would make or break the business.

 I picked a young guy, he was talented and level-headed, a family man, I gave him a "signing bonus" that I knew he'd plunk on a house (thereby tethering him to the job…). I wanted someone who was looking for a deal like that. I didn't need somebody who required close supervision or had one eye out for a different opportunity. The business of towing stayed low-key, I wasn't the kind of owner who pounded his shoe on the table.

 I had only one radical leaning and that was for criminalizing vehicular homicide to be the equal of any other life-taking. There were no impaired-driving *accidents*. There were homicidal decisions being made, electing a form of Russian Roulette played with a 3,000 pound bullet aimed at somebody else's head. For that, I say you pay with your life's time. I was surprised that other people didn't stand up and scream along with me. There is no justification for driving when you've hobbled your mind. If you want to cloud your vision, thicken your reactions, I don't have a problem with that as long as you do it out of my sight in the privacy of your own world. Don't bring it into my world or you pay the highest price for doing so.

I've got a little girl who is not going to learn not to run into the street for many more years. She has low impulse control and, even if those impulses are slow, they are capable of moving her. For a long time, she wouldn't chase a ball. She watched it until it stopped moving and then she decided to go to the ball. We used to sit across from each other with a hula hoop and roll a small ball back and forth in the circle, back and forth, for three years, before she learned to anticipate where the ball might go. More years before she moved beyond the hoop to standing and catching. So, until she actually absorbs the idea of not running into the street, she needs those few extra seconds that a competent driver can afford her. Don't we all?

I shop for Rose, I look through catalogs and find her labor-saving gadgets, I replace kitchen utensils, install organizer boxes in the laundry room, the subtext of each purchase is that I've watched her, I've had my eyes on her, and I have seen what she is doing. Or the improvements enhance my ability to participate. Every New Year's Eve, I pick out an outfit for her, something dressy, classy, for a night of ceremonial eating, drinking, dancing all leading to The Kiss of the New Year. That Kiss is one of our special things, it had started with grave courtesy when she was my grandmother's housemate, when we celebrated family style, but over the years we'd carved out a private night of wish-making to end one year and begin another.

It was fun for me to bumble around the dress shop; the clerks loved having a fashion acolyte to mold. It helped that Rose was a perfect size ten, her green eyes set the color palette, and I wanted her to feel stylish in it, not avant-garde, not cutting edge, she radiated the purest femininity and it deserved the proper wrapping. One year it was black silk, it whispered every time she moved. I'd provide the foundation garments, having learned different dresses require different underpinnings. It was my pleasure to set out the gift boxes the night before, so she could decide on jewelry, make-up. She prepared herself in private as I posed in my dinner jacket, anticipating her appearance. It was tradition that Mrs. D and Caroline were her ladies-in-waiting, organizing the beauty parade. I'd look up the steps and see Rose standing there, taking the dress I'd given her and making it her own. I was always surprised how much she added to the outfit each year. She grabbed my imagination and ran with it.

We loved walking out together, all dressed up; I had to slow down to match her high-heeled pace, it wasn't the most efficient mode of walking but she looked great doing it. She held my arm, pressed close, and I felt like a potentate. Beyond prince, above king... a monarch. The sight of this warm woman by my side gave me courage and dignity. My lady deserved a gentleman. I squired her that night, presenting her to the evening like a jewel in the palm of my hand. Rose and I left no room for doubt, we made the gestures, fulfilled the many aspects of marital love. Ushering in the New Year was a renewal through renegotiation. For all the laughter and giddiness, we also laid our plans for the coming year. We declared adjustments to our five-, ten- and twenty-year plans; after a night of lovemaking, we balanced the family books and projected our budget for the years to come.

We had breakfast courtesy of room service, eating in bed because the table was piled high with ledgers and receipts. We didn't have to argue about money, in the sense there was enough to go around, but we were naturally frugal people who didn't like to waste what we did have. We set targets for goods, clothing, utilities, not closing our eyes to the ongoing draining of our resources, we set goals for growing our security pile, and we looked ahead for each of the kids. There was no doubt we were both working for a living.

Jared was about to leave for college, we were all looking forward to this shift in residence. He'd outgrown himself in our house, he wanted to be free of the little boy we all remembered, college was going to be his hunting ground and there he'd aim for maturity. He never had the idea that college was free for him, he was expected to orchestrate his education with creativity, of course we'd be paying the lion's share but only after he had his portion to contribute. Taking real responsibility was a necessary element of his development. This put some of the weight on his shoulders.

Caroline was taking the Shore Store Redux too seriously for a girl almost sixteen, we wanted her to hire an assistant. She'd never heard of a teenager having an employee but we pointed out she declared profit from the Store so it was a legitimate tax-paying business. We convinced Caroline to get somebody else to help Mrs. D so she herself could concentrate on finishing high school, with extra time available to join a club or two, make the important connections with her tribal sisters. Rose was clear with me that girls were not all spices and nice, that there was a pecking order and it was established by vigorous pecking! Caroline shouldn't miss out on this rite of passage. The girl understood the merchant life, now it was time to live the student life.

I remember back to when Eileen was not yet on her feet, she was working up to it, the longer she crawled the happier we'd be, it was a patterning that seemed to benefit kids, quadrupedal locomotion hit the brain high and low, front and back, and represented a triumph for Eileen's learning to chain a behavior together. At first, she would move one of her four limbs then stop and figure out which limb should move next. Stop. Figure. Move. Stop. Figure. Move. She got smoother with the components but you could see it was all done in slow motion, frame by frame. Finally she began to blur the motions, sliding quicker from Stop to Move, in a repeating four-beat, and over time she picked up some speed. This was when we first noticed that she stopped before entering any room. Stopped. Figured. Moved. She interrupted the steady hand-knee hand-knee thing she had going to look at the bigger picture. She

Book II – Family. Life.

had grown comfortable crawling around any room she was in, but taking the next step, to feel comfortable moving between rooms, would take a while longer.

Think of the world from Eileen's point of view. People talk too fast, move too fast, write with too many symbols, have too many unspoken rules you are supposed to know by osmosis. Eileen wasn't big on osmosis, the culture was not imprinted on her between the lines of her school texts and common reading… she didn't know that there really were handsome Princes of England who could be the source of a living fairy tale, Jesus was as real to her as Santa Claus, neither of them trumped Mr. Rogers who soothed her twice a day. We think it was his predictability, but whatever it was, Eileen made it clear that seeing Mr. Rogers was a good thing. TV didn't much interest her otherwise, we found music was just as absorbing for her, so we presented variations on classical, R&B, and folk. For instance "Rock Around the Clock" had her dancing in a circle around an outsized clock-rug on the floor we used for time telling with her. She was miles away from correctly reading the hands for the hours and minutes for clues to her schedule but she knew when it was day-time and night-time. We started with the idea of 9-12-3-6 because that's how her day divided. 9 school 12 lunch 3 home 6 dinner. The shapes were distinct 🕘🕛🕒🕕 and limited to time telling. She understood "o'clock" literally because our clocks were round – we didn't introduce different shaped clock-faces until she mastered the big hour and little minute hands undistracted by the outline. TIME 🕐 CLOCK

All the Kids I'd known helped shape my appreciation for Eileen's style of learning, and vice versa. You need to look below the protective shell around a foster kid and figure out how to teach them to trust themselves. It seemed that I had been becoming acquainted with the mechanics of learning for some reason not then obvious to me but much appreciated now.

That's why I'm glad I have people who love me, and provide me with insight, like my Rose who asked if I was ever going to DO something constructive with my nervous energy without front-line towing. It turns out all my agitation was due to the fact I was hatching an idea. I saw two problems with the adult men associated with the Kids I knew, and the biggest pitfall for the Kids themselves: literacy and livelihood. You can bet they were linked. I decided to teach an elementary course in a mechanics workshop, a venue for supervised visits with probationary parents, else wise there were Big Brothers and Big Sisters to partner up with Kids (only at the garage, no off-site contact). We made our own maintenance manuals for recent model cars volunteered as a subject vehicle for the class. We looked at universal mechanical truths: precision matters, performance and components degrade over time, you can subdivide the car into ignition, engine, fuel, transmission, exhaust, wheels and brakes. We figured out each element. Then we typed it up, using the dictionary as required.

I knew it was not going to revolutionize every participant but it would hook a few, the ones who were looking to get caught, who figured out they could trade a forty-hour work week for one hundred twenty-eight hours of non-work liberation. Being poor made for a hundred sixty-eight hard hours a week. Skill-based trades were a fair deal for a person who will acquire the skill. Mechanics, hair stylists, health care aides, office work, jobs like these are places to plant a stake and start climbing the ladder, out of debt, up to solvency, and beyond. If the parent "passed" our six-week course, they were assured it would be worth the money to get their certificate at the trade school. If it turned out they were all thumbs at the car stuff, at least it was a lesson learned for free. The Kids that volunteered for the class were credited with hours having the same value as homework or chores, self-improvement and community involvement contributions. There was latitude in what you could do but none regarding how much of it you should do. Ten hours a week of self-improvement or community involvement. Thirty-five for school. Ten for homework/brain stimulus. Six hours of Energy Expenditure (fitness or sport). We had do-it-yourself home repair classes. Writing clubs. Mathletes. It all worked to the benefit of the group by strengthening the individuals. Their responsibilities stacked straight across from their rewards, no hidden tariff. Room clean, you get phone time. Homework done, you get game time. Duty hours traded for free hours.

This philosophy provided continuity as the Kids Place evolved, kids came and went, some stayed, but we had to remain prepared to provide safety to children in flux. Primal powers moved in their fates, abandonment, abuse, indifference, haplessness. Even so... Even so. That was the bridging phrase to discussions of how things worked in the Kids Place. There were no exceptions to being held accountable. The only way to build up any brownie points was to stay current with your obligations, then the extra effort could be accumulated for a better reward. Scared, mad, dull, all the same – here's how you get what you want. It was a form of obedience training, the difference is that they were mastering themselves.

Once in a while we worked with a parent who was on the verge of success, who was having quality visitation, showing stability of residence and employment, learning how to use the system to fill in the gaps between an honest day's labor and a good night's sleep. The family unit had a much greater chance to maintain itself if the kid was a contributing member of the dynamic. The kid should not be sucking up the parent's energy fighting over homework or hygiene, these were the duties of all humans, just do it. A small group who chooses to work together for their mutual benefit can amplify their power through efficiency. Team work is a sign of intelligence, creating a division of self and other, and the uniting of us. Family-style living, one for all.

Jared was seeking an identity among his peers by figuratively playing for a team other than his family. His allegiance to his age-mates was incredible, he had a strong sense of solidarity with his pals and, to them, it seemed the world existed to thwart their innocent plans. They were oblivious, uncaring of other people's feelings, and hoped those others viewed their behavior with the same disregard: why were grownups so *interested* in the actions of their teenagers? You go your (old) way and they'll go their (new) way... they naively presume because all their feelings are new to them that those are sharper than our feelings, but that isn't so. Whatever rush of discovery experienced in the teens is honed in subsequent years so that a richness of intent is possible. Ardor is easy when your engine runs hot like it does for the teens, it's a trickier business when you have to prime the pump but all the more precious. There's a reason the torch passes, there are keepers of the flame and carriers of the flame, both are required by the flame.

The flame is life, teens dance in the flicker, not realizing they can snuff their own wick. The eternal flame goes on, but that one light goes out. O.U.T. not-coming-back gone. The fact is we are like other herds who lose a certain percentage of their offspring to predators and misfortune. We lose some of our teens, culling the vulnerable and the reckless, although we don't like to say it that way. Every biological sequence has breakpoints and you can see the flurry of death begin in the 15-24 year-old human bracket. (The sweet spot is ages 5-14, where the smallest percentage of death occurs per thousand.[1]) Children rarely slip out of life, they are wrenched, jerked, snatched away from their expectations of years to come. There are few natural ways for a child to lose their life. Death is a disease, death stalks, it is not (yet) inherent in their systems. Death grows on us over time, we get familiar with the slowing process, carry the weight of experience until it wears us down... elders are further along the trail and can look back a far distance, hinting what is in front of us all. We are our grandparents' grandchildren, our children are our parent's grandchildren. The rise and fall of a wave of souls, people incarnated on the one same day out of the countless eternity of them. Great grandpa had a horse, grandpa had a wagon, dad had a car, you've got an SUV, and your kid is on a motorcycle. It's all the same, isn't it? You're on the move in the mode of the day but where you go and why you go there is the tale of your life.

---

1   http://www.disastercenter.com/cdc/
From 1-4 the death rate per 100,000 people is 38.3
From 5- 14 the death rate per 100,000 people is 22
From 15- 24 the death rate per 100,000 people is 90.3
From 25- 44 the death rate per 100,000 people is 177.8
From 45- 64 the death rate per 100,000 people is 708
For people over 65 the death rate per 100,000 people is 5,071.40

Book II – Family. Life.

Sports car people share the highway with minivan drivers, different itineraries, same pavement. Our cranky teens have to share the planet, as much as it pains them, and running smack dab into the actuality of your life is a rite of passage. Your actual adult life exerts limits, you have a certain amount of resources, that has to translate to survival at a level you agree to maintain. Teens don't have the capacity they will ultimately have as adults, even if some come into their own sooner or more completely. Their larger size can be confusing, there are connections missing in teen thinking and as their guardian you need to supply those. Jared is a good kid but he's still a kid and I have to counsel myself to patience.

It helps if I remember my own teen-age foolishness, how proud I was of myself when I wasn't filled with self-doubt and loathing. The times were simpler back then, of course, but even in light of my peers' world, mine was one step back, a lot quieter, because I lived with my Grandma and her husband Carl. I had no siblings. My mother was not there to bridge the two generations so I had to figure it all out for myself. I did, however, miss the primal confrontation of parent-teen, everything was formalized elder-youth for me. I was grateful sometimes for the built-in easement, especially when I figured out the situations of some of my friends who were controlled by, how shall we say, negative adult role models? The truth was, there were fewer traditional families in my circle than there were the single parent & kid(s) combo. Ironically, the worst situation I saw was an only child who was too important to her parents, they lived through her, scheduled their work around her school events, were snack captains for the baseball team and drivers for the church field trips. She was rarely allowed to act on her own, they chaperoned her to and from all her activities. It wasn't even carpooling, she was the honored cargo and it was her agenda that drove them, they would gladly drive anybody else's kid but nobody else drove their kid. She was unsure of herself when they weren't there, something I didn't notice until Grandma pointed it out. Grandma knew my friends and classmates but she kept a respectful distance, fulfilling her volunteer obligations and then stepping back. It was a great comfort to me to know Grandma and Carl were where they always were doing what they always did. That's what I tried to give Jared, he could count on me to be me.

The patience was run-off from my interaction with little Eileen. I'd wiped all the development handbooks out of my mind and concentrated on engaging her, sensing that she needed people to make the effort to reach her, she would watch but not act. I devoted myself to providing her a more vigorous sense of interaction. I had to work hard not to lead her, the purpose of many of her actions wasn't readily apparent to others. She and I would make faces, mimic sounds, repeat the "head, heart, hands" gestures, I balanced this intense focus with hauling her around on my errands, taking her to the paint store, to get the truck lubed, there was no way I was going to deny her the world.

She learned to cope, tapping her fingers together when she was nervous, she would watch them tap-tap-tap-tap-tap-tap if things got too chaotic. Traffic was beyond her consideration, being in the car, in her car seat, was stimulus enough. I kept things simple, giving her time to get oriented to each change. In the car, out of the car, in the store, out of the store. Caroline told me she thinks of her sister as a slow processor, it takes her longer to sort out what she sees and hears and feels, and when it piles up unprocessed she gets agitated. Give her time to sort herself out and she did fine. Patience.

Since I was doing less road work, I had more time on my hands. I'd delegated the Kids Place "building society" to a graduate-resident, a good guy from a bad home, letting him provide for other kids filled in the hole left by his own confused boyhood. He was a living example to current residents that people can stay the course and emerge survivors. He and I talked on the phone often, bouncing around ideas, we were simpatico on the basic maintenance plan so the place stayed in trim (we weren't trying to manicure it). The Kids saw how things got done, you learned to make a bed, set a table, sweep a floor, dust, mop, dust mop, vacuum. Any money we saved on having a maintenance crew went to Entertainment (movie tickets, skating, picnic lunch for a hike). It was a real education to some of the kids who'd never taken care of themselves.

Book II – Family. Life.

Rose communicated with Eileen in her own way (tender-tough), I was surprised how silly they got sometimes, the biggest element was tangency, they were in touch, Rose held Eileen, then stretched out next to her, then sat across from her, crawled alongside. They were obviously mother-daughter, Jared and Caroline were her blood kin too. I looked like I was Eileen's dad. No matter how involved I got, however, Eileen had imprinted her primary love on Rose – a move I could understand completely.

Rose also cracked the code on Eileen's tantrums. Like all toddlers, our little angel had to learn to exert her will with dignity and she had the usual violent reactions to being told No. Rose got simpler as Eileen got madder. Eileen would ratchet up from simple head shaking to a neck-stiffening, feet-drumming, scream-a-thon. Rose would turn full focus on Eileen's feelings, participate in her anger, and absorb it. "Eileen mad! Eileen fighting! No! Eileen says No!"

Rose said out loud what she saw her daughter *feeling*. That gave Eileen time to learn the words. Once she had the words we could work on the volume. We both believed Eileen would find herself frustrated in life. She was able to understand ideas before she could articulate them, and there were going to be gaps between what she saw other people have and what she could have. (Like all of us.) She'd be harder to console because she did indeed face a hard road. Jared mourned her lost independence, he was busy grabbing for his and it hurt him to see that she would never drive, never live alone… not like he would, not like Caroline. Life wasn't fair. I agreed that was the fact. Get over it. Take what you got and go with it before it's gone.

Eileen reshuffled our deck, Rose took an executive advisor role at Kids Place, hiring two people to do her old job. She wouldn't want that day-to-day responsibility back, whatever came next wouldn't be the same. Just like me, she felt her life had changed with the arrival of our daughter. Not only her goals but her pace. As a couple, we were solid. Fidelity, romance, pride. As parents, we pledged to our fledglings. We had the home front covered, agreeing that, still, there was unmet need in the world, perhaps we could help somehow. We always liked our contribution to be tangible, we didn't write checks to faceless charity boards. We weren't quite ready to initiate contact but we were looking for a cause.

Mrs. D was standing up against a diagnosis of Alzheimer's, having time to prepare her estate to cushion her future, knowing we'd be on the look-out for her as always. She and Eileen were eerily similar as Mrs. D lost track of current days, she found Eileen the least changeable of us all and they spent their time together sorting fabric for the charity quilting bee, listening to Raffi sing silly songs. Mrs. D was a good woman who had enjoyed an interesting life. She was sorry to see glimpses of her end, she still hoped to pop out in her sleep... all her life, transitions had been confusing and drawn-out. She was formed by war, redeemed by commerce, fulfilled by us, the family who enfolded her. Caroline was too young to take on the Shore Store alone so the two of them interviewed then engaged a business manager, a recent accounting school graduate who would be sending part of his paycheck to his mother to feed his brothers and sisters. We bought him a health policy that covered everybody in his family, plus provided him a company station wagon, handy for hauling supplies, doubling as his family lifeline for transportation. Putting money in his hands was a big step for all of us, it seemed smart to put some of his compensation in tangible form. We bought a condo and he rebated a portion of his salary as rent to have a retreat from the world. It was too small to house his family, and that was no accident on our part. We wanted him to be on his own, free to reach back and help the others, but investing in himself to maximize his potential, thereby enriching his many working years to come. Caroline was in high school and was taking time out to be a girl. It relieved Mrs. D who found herself less and less sure of her surroundings, she was going to pull herself inward, she felt she would do best with a small simple room in a rectilinear arrangement with other similar rooms, a senior facility with memory care. Our house was too big, too busy, and it made her feel anxious. She liked to play the radio softly and she couldn't *hear* it when all these strangers tromped through the house. Young Caroline, the old Mrs. D, an apprentice accountant and I worked

Book II – Family. Life.

our brains together to make sure the Store held true to its charter. Great stuff at good prices.

The power of the mind should stupefy us. It runs the autonomic systems in the background then monitors variant systems in the foreground. Breathing is autonomic, but inhaling the scent of a flower is consciously controlled. We calculate everything (even intangibles). Value. Assigning it. Acquiring it. Rose and I were seeing that as the metaphor for progress: discover what you value and pursue it. Learn to value virtues as well as assets, own your emotional self. That let us see that Jared did have a soul, under his metal-band hair and Rebel Without a Clue philosophy, he was a mish-mash of bravado and impetuosity, he was eager for the zing of emotional battles. Typical teen. He was assembling his escape pod and laying in supplies for his solo venture. That's how he and I talked about his approaching manhood. I laid it on the line, whether you get your money writing songs or digging ditches is your business, but you better be prepared to pay for food, shelter and every other dang thing you wanted. I didn't let him distract me with his grandiose plans for making millions, I looked over want ads with him and let him see what places cost to rent, not in my humble opinion, but in fact, here, now. We got insurance quotes for his dream car and then scaled it down to something he could afford. That plus his car payment had to be calculated as survival money because he could not conceive of life without a car! Rather than argue the point, I let him compare prices and features until he approached the sweet spot of a good car he could afford to insure. That was going to be his pod. It wasn't easy for us to let him go, we knew so many more things than we had the time to tell him: what to watch for, how to smell a rat. Rather than fighting his first steps out of our house, we opened our arms, like Rose did when he was learning to walk, knowing he was going to fall but understanding it was the only way for him to learn to stay up on his own two feet. Letting him learn that lesson increased his chance of survival even if it loosened his mother's literal hold on him.

Rose and I blended our memories, to create a stronger bond. We'd agreed to create a world together from the materials we'd collected so far in life. It was a merger, not a buy-out (on either side). Marriage is a trainer airplane, both sides need full control in extreme situations. We weren't doing a Leader-Follower deal, we were abreast.

I'm toying with the idea of a business model to structure a new venture. I believe you can impose a financial accounting system on any vendor-based business to better its performance, getting to the bedrock of the income and outgo, stripping away the wasted motions and lost advantages, creating partnerships between money people and service people. Maximize earnings by minimizing expenses. Invest in efficiencies. Parcel out the responsibilities for making the business work. A good carpenter doesn't earn money standing on-line at the bank, that's a different world. Keep him with the wood, the tools, the dreams.

Car repair. Construction services. Whenever you had somebody selling goods or time/skill, money changed hands. Get somebody who knows money like you know how to do what you do and you'll improve your outcome. Cultivate a formal view of your business, share it with somebody who is motivated to see you succeed because their income depends on it. Make sure you pick somebody to handle your money who understands you're going to audit them as a condition of the partnership. You establish yourself as dead serious because you're not ready to advance if you don't believe that of yourself. I decided I would be a business matchmaker, getting to know who was looking for what. I wouldn't be charging for the match-ups, those were free. I hosted a gathering every six weeks where likely candidates mingled. It was partly a Public Speaking course because each attendee sketched their business background and interests. I served tidy food, no alcohol, invited experts in various fields to make themselves available, and all it cost was $25 at the door which I gave to the meeting hall. (My foregone salary made this possible.) The idea was to provide a stocked pond, identifying individuals who were ready to kick up production of the goods/services if only they could get out from behind their desks. Paperwork is the bane of invention, for some. For others, it's boon.

The Home Helper we hired understood the job was holistic, Eileen required a stronger routine than most charges, and the house was as much

Book II – Family. Life.

a living entity as any family member. We had periodic cleaning parties, yard work parties, closet organizing parties. Everybody got involved, it was part of the tariff for using the house. It kept us in touch with each other, doing familiar things, working through the moods of that particular day, joking and poking at each other in our raggediest clothes. After the job was done, we all took showers and then went out to dinner together. These were the bonds that held when the emotional battles got heated. These recurring projects were so much a part of our family life that even in the worst mood you were not excused from communal chores, it is what you did if you lived there. You work. You shower. You dine. Prizing routine is the natural result of my growing up with Grandma and Carl, and their influence was felt in the next generation. Rose was our captain, she picked the chore and set the goal. Whatever we could get done in two hours would be done. An hour to shower. Ninety minutes to dine (including travel). Scheduling a nice dinner at five made it easier for our younger members, they could practice good manners and still get home in time for outings with their friends, we could scoot out to a movie. We cleared out of the restaurants before the serious diners arrived. The Home Helper was a binding element in the household, recruited to fill in our gaps, stand in for us, advocate the outside opinion. This wasn't an easy job but it wasn't hard either, it was something that was developed for mutual benefit. In many ways, we were richer for spending the money to have help.

The part-time nannies also provided light housekeeping if it was part of Eileen's schedule. They worked with her doing chores, just like they ate with her if it was meal time. The overall plan let Eileen's need dominate the house without overburdening any one person. It can be grueling to parent a kid with special needs, it seemed natural that Rose would turn her professional eye towards easing that burden for others once she'd figured out a system for us. Eileen had mild impairments, Rose was more worried about kids who were in need of physical assistance, she saw the county overburdened by parents who didn't have the first clue as to how to help themselves. She figured she could work directly with the parents, coordinating their applications for benefits, hooking them up with support groups and free classes, involving herself in their enrichment. She wouldn't dealt directly with the children, this was parental outreach, she had corporate sponsorship so they had two classrooms, four offices, a gymnasium. One end of the gym was netted so the littlest kids could lose themselves in oblivious play while the older kids were shooting baskets or playing volleyball. Mom/Dad/Auntie filled out forms, registered for services while the kids were tended by apprentice babysitters, just like we had done at the Clinic long ago, creating a system for the whole family.

We were a wellness clinic, our services were not for the desperate, they were for parents who had decided to pick up the reins and drive their family forward, they weren't dodging the truth about whichever kid(s) in the family needed extra help. By educating themselves about options, they were better advocates for state assistance, and they took advantage of the best parts of our social system. Their kids got sleeker wheelchairs, more efficient vaporizers, longer tutoring, and best of all they got stronger families. There were cross-over cases who started with Rose and then entered my business circle in order to better themselves. It is amazing what a bit of support can do for a family experiencing the wobbles. We didn't have a religious agenda, or even a lifestyle preference for the families. We wanted them to establish their own standards as we helped them secure that for themselves.

Eileen was around five years old when she christened herself one of the Sleepy People. We're not sure where she picked up the phrase, and could only guess at what she thought that meant, but she applied it to Down Syndrome people and others who were visibly retarded. She did not apply it to people with palsy. Old people were Sleepy People, pregnant women were Sleepy People and infants were included, too. I think she lumped all "awake" people into a mysterious phalanx of raw power. They marched up to her and past her without absorbing her.

Knowing we weren't going to have any more kids helped Rose and I maintain a scintillating love life, we made love only for the pleasure. We tried not to act goofy in public, having relaxed after years together. In the beginning we were avid for each other's personal attention. We don't like it any less, we're just more secure about its delivery.

I had decided that I wanted to be known as the man with the happy wife. The measure of my marriage was in the progress of my spouse and myself. I thought men who abandoned their women and children were lesser than those of us who reached out to our people. Still, these were subjective values. The idea that Rose should be inconvenienced, let alone suffer, for my behavior was ludicrous. It was as simple as that for us. We did each other proud. We were considerate and found that to be a stimulating basis for continued involvement. Some of Starlight's Peace and Love ran through me, to be sure, but I also had Grandma's sense of beauty, Carl's sense of duty. I hold my life dear to me, and by extension I believe that every life is tender and in need of nurture. Without love of self, there is no appreciation of other. I want to be remembered for my thoughtfulness expressed through action. I want my loved ones to feel my devotion, beyond my presence. I have taken my stance, struggle to hold it, to show them I am worthy.

Back Story

Kathleen K. has created a library of Private Publications available at KathleenKBooks.com. Her eclectic collection features narrative fiction centered on family life in The Lent Hand (Adventures in Beach Town Towing), literate erotica (Dark Prince, Heed Thy Queen) and the counterculture fictional memoir of Stoner with a Boner (It's a Long Story).

Transplanted to the Pacific Northwest, Kathleen K is a product of the small press/poetry culture with a background in alternative publishing. Her vivid use of language captures characters while life itself provides the twists and turns.

Her non-fiction book Sweet Talkers (Words from the Mouth of a Pay-to-Say Girl) is the true chronicle of a phone-sex business, now considered a cult classic. The book is out of print but never out of style. Intended for adults only, <u>Sweet Talkers</u> is available on-line as a collectible. Second edition Spring 2012.

The rest of her work is make-believe. She makes you believe she's a tow truck driver who falls in love with a shattered family. She makes you believe she's a grocer with an after-hours fondness for pot and sex. She makes you believe she's an accountant hijacked in her car after work and ordered to Drive North.

Kathleen K. drops readers into situations as diverse as the world of Honey B., Sexual Consultant, and of Baby Girl Battersea, fatherless heir to a family fortune in the clutches of her selfish uncle. These books are not linked by theme or genre, this is a rich collection of all-age and adults-only offerings comprising decades of production.

Sharp dialog, elegant prose and a sassy attitude give the audience credit for reading between the lines. Consistently praised for her ability to capture tone and emotion, Kathleen K. is a strong voice in contemporary fiction.

Becoming available for the first time in print and e-book format, these Private Publications are varied in topic but easily identifiable as Words Arranged by Kathleen K.